He Hadn't Come Back To Hear Her Life Story.

He already knew that drive, anger and fear made up ambition; he'd already guessed that Kathryn had learned about all of those too young. He'd come back to find out if there was a chance she ever stood motionless.

She saw Grant coming toward her and could have cursed herself for letting down her guard. Never mind. Once he discovered what it was like to kiss a chip of ice, he'd back off.

Exactly then, his mouth covered hers. Like the rush of a wave the kiss kept coming, building up tension and power and momentum with evocative speed.

When she stood still as a statue, his lips lifted from hers.

Why couldn't she have been ice? "I..." Her tongue felt thick. She couldn't think of a thing to say.

"Fun, wasn't it?"

Dear Reader,

Welcome to Silhouette! Our goal is to give you hours of unbeatable reading pleasure, and we hope you'll enjoy each month's six new Silhouette Desires. These sensual, provocative love stories are both believable and compelling—sometimes they're poignant, sometimes humorous, but always enjoyable.

Indulge yourself. Experience all the passion and excitement of falling in love along with our heroine as she meets the irresistible man of her dreams and together they overcome all obstacles in the path to a happy ending.

If this is your first Desire, I hope it'll be the first of many. If you're already a Silhouette Desire reader, thanks for your support! Look for some of your favorite authors in the coming months: Stephanie James, Diana Palmer, Dixie Browning, Ann Major and Doreen Owens Malek, to name just a few.

Happy reading!

Isabel Swift
Senior Editor

SDRL-7/85

JENNIFER GREENE
Minx

Silhouette Desire

Published by Silhouette Books New York

America's Publisher of Contemporary Romance

SILHOUETTE BOOKS
300 East 42nd St., New York, N.Y. 10017

Copyright © 1987 by Jennifer Greene

ISBN: 0-373-05366-5

First Silhouette Books printing July 1987

America's Publisher of Contemporary Romance

Printed in the U.S.A.

Books by Jennifer Greene

Silhouette Desire

Body and Soul #263
Foolish Pleasure #293
Madam's Room #326
Dear Reader #350
Minx #366

JENNIFER GREENE

lives near Lake Michigan. Born in Grosse Pointe, she moved to a farm when she married her husband fifteen years ago. Jennifer feels that love needs both laughter and tribulations to grow. She's won the *Romantic Times* award for Sensuality and the RWA Silver Medallion, and also writes under the name of Jeanne Grant.

One

Kathryn was ready to personally carry Michigan's Upper Peninsula to the middle of the Pacific Ocean and drop it in.

June heat steamed in her enclosed car. A pickup barreling down the opposite side of the road had slushed another bucket of water on her windshield. The rain hadn't let up in hours, and the road was like a pitted water slide. To a camper, the landscape of endless woods and protected wilderness was undoubtedly fascinating, but Kathryn had seen enough drooping, dripping trees to last a lifetime.

Michigan could have its Water Wonderland. She wanted Chicago, and for the past eight hours of driving she'd worried about nothing but Chicago. Saturday was the store's busiest day. What if Spence hadn't shown up for work? Bess couldn't handle it alone. Decisions had to be made about the winter line. The lawyer who owned the property was ranting about another rent increase.

She simply couldn't be gone, not for eight hours and definitely not for two weeks. After five long years, the store was finally in the black and thriving, but competition for a woman's fashion dollar was fierce in downtown Chicago. Success could slip away in the blink of an eye. She'd worked too hard, sacrificed too much, paid too many prices, to let that happen.

Anxiety pounded in her temples. The headache was so familiar that she ignored it ... and then nearly missed the faded sign for Silverwater.

Three minutes later she shot a dry glance at the rearview mirror. She'd seen three bars, a grocery store and a fishing tackle shop. So much for Silverwater. Her fingers fumbled for the makeshift map on the passenger seat. Five more miles north, then three miles west ...

By the time she turned down the last potholed road, the rain had slowed down to a nerve-racking drizzle. Her raspberry silk blouse and jeans were permanently stuck to her skin. Her stomach was grumbling to the same beat as her headache, and there was a definite chance she would have sold her soul for a tall, cold glass of iced tea. Preferably peppermint.

The devil was obviously uninterested in buying souls today. The last road ended abruptly—in a lakelike mud puddle. Just beyond was a rustic log cabin liberally surrounded by thriving weeds and nestled in more wet, sagging woods. A bedraggled-looking porch went around the front. The place defined gloom. She hadn't expected much, but the twenty-acre inheritance from Uncle Toby was supposed to carry the title of Mink Ranch.

She saw no sign of the minks, or of anything civilized enough to justify the term "ranch." This whole business was upsetting. Toby had been the black sheep of the family; she'd only met her uncle once as a very little girl. He must have intended the inheritance as a kindness, but darn it, it wasn't. She didn't want the property or have any idea what to do with it.

Ever since the lawyer had contacted her about her uncle's death, guilt had been gnawing at her, not because of this dilapidated "windfall," but because of her uncle. He'd severed all contact with the family years before, and he'd certainly never shown any interest in or care for her. Still, he must have been a lonely man, isolated up here in these weed-infested woods. Maybe he'd needed someone. Maybe he'd needed a niece. She hadn't even known his address until he'd died.

She'd grown up believing that one could always find time for people, for caring. Her values hadn't changed, but her life-style had. Lately she couldn't beg borrow or steal a free minute. There had to be a way off the lonely roller coaster track of responsibility, pressure and tension, and this twenty-acre white elephant was *not* helping. She needed a mink ranch like she needed warts.

Biting her lip, she reached into the back for her leather purse and Gucci overnight bag. Her sandals sank in the mud the instant she stepped out of the car. The cabin was supposed to be unlocked, and if it wasn't she'd break a window to get in. Enough was enough, and that went for the mental complaining as well. She'd handle it. She'd handle all of it. With a little drive, a little determination and a lot of just plain stubbornness, she'd smoothed over problems worse than this.

Gingerly she lifted a mud-ridden sandal and took the first step toward the ramshackle porch. The man suddenly appearing from the woods did a marvelous job of nearly scaring her out of her wits.

At first glance he impressed her as only having recently been let out of a cage. Well-worn jeans molded over muscular legs. His plaid shirt was frayed, and his beard was a vagrant scrawl of black hair sprinkled with silver. Raven brows perched over dark emotive eyes. The rumpled mass of hair hadn't seen a barber in ages. His square features were sun-bronzed and strong-boned to match a frame that could have made a gangster learn manners.

There was a remote possibility that if he were cleaned up and tamed, some women might have found him extraordinarily good-looking. Brawn and beards weren't Kathryn's cup of tea. Neither were rough diamonds. What's more, his sassy black eyes looked dangerous.

She mentally sighed, then fastened on her best civilized smile. "Hello there! You must be a neighbor of my uncle's?"

He stopped. "I'm Grant Kaufman, yes."

Well, terrific. Sort of. Kaufman's name headed the list in her purse—he was the neighbor who'd been taking care of the animals since her uncle's death. His showing up certainly saved her having to track him down. Somehow, though, she'd assumed the man would be a kindly old codger of her uncle's vintage, not a backwoods vagrant with sexy eyes and an arrogant grin.

Juggling her night case and purse, she maneuvered in the mud-slick yard so she could extend a manicured white hand. "I'm Kathryn Price. I wrote you I was coming? And I apologize for leaving you with the responsibility of the animals this past week, but very honestly this was the soonest I could get here."

"I never received your letter—haven't been into town to pick up my mail—but it doesn't matter. I didn't mind caretaking the creatures."

Her hand was swallowed by his paw. Calluses grated against her more tender flesh, and his skin was Indian dark next to her city pale. The power of his handshake affected her less than the searing lance of those dark eyes. With annoying boldness, his gaze swept the mold of her blouse to her stretch of long legs, then dawdled on her mouth and drifted to the tired smudges beneath her eyes.

Pulling away her hand, she immediately stepped back. The impact of his lazy smile had her heart skipping beats, which struck her as the most humorous thing that had happened all day. At thirty-one she certainly recognized chemistry when she felt it, and one bad marriage hadn't soured her on men. She liked men just fine. When they behaved.

Getting rid of Devil-Eyes wasn't going to take long. "Well, now..." She strived for a tone of voice no warmer than the North Sea. "I'm glad it was so easy to find you. And I hate to bother you, but I was hoping you'd be willing to answer a few questions for me."

"Sure." An amused smile peeked out of that beard.

Maybe he had nothing better to do than stand there and look huge. Out of patience, Kathryn moved swiftly toward the cabin. "First, obviously I need to know where the minks are, how I'm supposed to take care of them, what they're fed and so on. And if you could tell me if there's anyone who deals in real estate in town? And money, Mr. Kaufman. Uncle Toby's lawyer gave me your name, but I never really understood if you were a friend or just a neighbor of my uncle's. Regardless, I hope you weren't worried I'd take advantage of that relationship. I'll be glad to pay you for the work you've had to do for the animals..."

Her brisk tone trailed off as she pushed open the cabin door and dropped her bags inside. She almost forgot the man when she glanced at the interior. A perfectly terrible day took an additional nosedive. Kathryn usually wasn't the kind to cave in over a little trouble, but the temptation was now definitely there.

Stifling heat and humidity reeked in the closed space. Dust coated the windows, and the rag-tail carpet on the floor had never seen a vacuum cleaner. To her left, cracked vinyl chairs surrounded a Formica table that was sticky with grime. Beyond was a kitchen ell, with a squat, rusty refrigerator and a dauntingly unfamiliar cookstove. No counters. The stained sink had a hand pump, and the peeling wallpaper had some pattern with guns and Indians on it, the type found in 1950s boys' bedrooms.

The main room had log walls, and the old stone fireplace might have had some potential for charm if the ashes in the grate weren't eight inches deep. A choice of kerosene lanterns sat on the mantle, each competing for a prize in dinginess. Bookshelves were jammed helter-skelter. The long leather couch was the room's one claim to decent furniture, if and when it received some direct contact with soap and water. She noted the open sleeping loft, but couldn't give it more than a glance. Undoubtedly it was just as unlivable as the rest of the place.

"A little rough and tumble," murmured the dry tenor behind her. "I've had access to the place since I've been watching over the minks, so I guess you can blame me for the shape it's in. If you want to know the truth, I didn't think I had the right to touch anything."

"Of course I don't blame you. It wasn't your responsibility." She turned to him with a smile that could have used a brace to support it. "Obviously my uncle didn't consider housekeeping much of a priority. Did you know him well?''

Grant shook his head. "No one knew him well. Toby kept to himself. He liked it that way. I took care of his animals when he had to be away or was laid up. He paid me back with a cord of wood, a string of fish, whatever he wanted." Studying her face, he said quietly, "My guess is you'll find some mosquito netting and a sleeping bag in the loft. I'll get it for you if you want. You can make up a bed on the porch and worry about the rest of this tomorrow."

"Thanks, but I'll handle it from here." She'd never sleep two seconds with the place as it was—never mind the headache slicing through her temples. Postponed problems only got bigger.

"If you'd like some help—"

"No, really, I can handle it. It's not your problem." For at least five years her body had been coaxed, bullied and pushed into giving her a second wind. All she had to do was talk herself out of being tired.

"That old stove's a little touchy, particularly if you've never seen one like it."

"I'll manage." She didn't mean to sound short, but she was breathless. After moving briskly to the first window and battling with the sash, she threw it open. "The only thing I'm really worried about is the animals. I've never even seen a mink, much less have any idea how to take care of one. As fast as you can, fill me in, then I won't bother you any longer."

The irritating man leaned against the inside wall and lazily crossed his legs. "You drove straight through from Chicago?"

"Yes." Ignoring him, she moved to a second window. At the same time as she opened it, she tugged the holey shade from its roller. Trash bag material.

"Some might want to relax a little after a drive like that before they slipped into high gear."

"Some might," she agreed. By the time she opened the fifth and last window, she'd seen a wealth of weeds from four directions. "Do you know if Uncle Toby had some kind of mower or tools? And there must be a store around here where I can buy some supplies. Lord, even a broom. Anything."

"Most stores will be closed by now, but there's a bar down the road that serves some pretty good food if you're hungry."

"I brought enough food to last a day or two. And a few supplies as well." Kathryn believed in being prepared, but there was no way she could be prepared for this. Everywhere she looked there was disaster.

"You want help bringing things in?"

"No, but thanks."

Grant expected the answer. At first glance he'd labeled her a duchess, and nothing she'd done since had changed that impression. The lady was a beauty from her sleek long legs to her pampered skin. From the sweep of ash-blond hair to the cool blue eyes and regal profile, he knew the type.

Her makeup was flawless. She reeked efficiency. She came from somewhere with manicured lawns and

chilled Perrier and looked ready to organize everything within sight using superb managerial skill. She
moved with constant frenetic energy, and her hands
never stayed still. He could see the pallor of real exhaustion beneath her makeup, the smudge of mauve
shadows under her eyes. She was thin. She obviously
never indulged in anything like lemon meringue pies,
assuming she remembered to eat at all.

He didn't even know her, and the look of her exasperated him. Once upon a time he'd known Kathryn,
or a lot of women just like her. She came from that
world of rush-rush and ulcers, of driving purpose and
early heart attacks that he'd left five years ago.

Grant hadn't missed that world since. Absently
rubbing an itch between his shoulder blades against
the log wall, he felt amusement as he watched her hide
an increasing look of frustration. There was nothing
to hurry for here. Silence, woods, peace, no schedules and not a damn thing for her to manage. He figured she wouldn't last a day without going stark-raving
mad.

"Mr. Kaufman?" Exasperated, Kathryn placed her
hands on her hips. So far he'd asked her questions, but
he certainly hadn't answered any.

"Grant," he corrected smoothly.

"Well, Grant, then." His token offers of help were
nice, but she didn't want any. Owing people was dangerous, and Kathryn didn't expect other people to
share her responsibilities. All she wanted from the man
was some answers and then to be left alone. Instead,
he appeared to be installed against her wall; Kathryn

figured he could fall asleep standing up. If there was anything that irritated her in a man, it was a look of laziness. "At least, would you show me the minks?" she finally asked.

He hesitated. "In the morning."

"I had in mind now," she said, then tacked on, "if you wouldn't mind."

"That's really not a good idea. They've been fed for the day. No need for you to tackle them until tomorrow, and I'll be around then to show you the ropes."

"There'll be no need to bother you in the morning if you show me now," she said reasonably. Again he hesitated. She couldn't fathom why and wasn't sure why she was being quite so abrupt, except that she desperately wanted to be alone. Her neighbor disturbed her; she wasn't too proud to admit it.

"Suit yourself," he said finally.

She'd love to. Following the brawny pair of shoulders outside and around to the back of the cabin, she considered that it would also suit her to set a firecracker beneath him. His loping gait was more appropriate for a picnic than for getting down to business. As far as she could tell, he was leading them into a brambly thicket of overgrown trees and brush. Everything was dripping from the rain, and the weeds were a mile high. She slapped a pesky mosquito hovering around her neck. He turned at the sound.

"Insects will probably bother you less if you leave off with that fancy perfume," he said mildly. "Blackflies are really strong this year, worse than the mosquitoes. Indians used to cover themselves with bear grease, which is still probably the best repellent there is."

He was obviously putting her on. "I'll be glad to borrow some from a bear next time I run into one."

"Not likely to run into bears around here these days. Wolves, though—we still have plenty of wolves at night. Bobcats, too."

She stopped dead, and then deliberately quickened her step, darting a wry glance at his back. All right. He'd labeled her a city slicker. That's exactly what she was, and he could revel in this mosquito-packed, uncivilized, sprawling wilderness until doomsday with her blessing.

"Watch it now." He held back the low tree branch so she could pass, then let it go, just fast enough so that she felt the whiplash spatter her back with water. A few droplets drizzled down her neck. He smiled. So, determinedly, did Kathryn.

"Isn't this lovely? So natural and—" she had to think of the appropriate word "—untamed."

"Like it, do you?"

She glanced at him sharply. Those dark eyes stared back at her with the innocent gentleness of a deer. "It's definitely a change from where I live." Where she lived there was air-conditioning, frozen daiquiris, showers and an apartment done in cool peach colors where someone else worried about the landscaping. "It's definitely different here," she repeated.

"And you haven't seen the minks yet. I'm sure you're going to feel really enthusiastic about those, Kate."

"Kathryn," she corrected automatically.

The intense jungle—she refused to call it a path—finally gave way to a miniature clearing. He headed directly for the strange-looking building. The structure was long and low, with a shake-shingled roof and dozens of small windows on each side. Two silver maples shaded the place. For the first time since she'd arrived, Kathryn took heart. The weeds were mowed, and the building looked clean, neat and sound, much more what she'd expected.

"Your uncle's specialty was silvers, you know."

"Silvers?"

"Silver minks. Actually, they're called Silver Blu in the business. He's got about a hundred Silvers and close to thirty Topaze—they're what I'd call a caramel color. Your uncle bred for the fancy colors. The more rare the color, the more valuable the pelt. You own a fur coat?" He pulled open the door for her.

"No," she said shortly. "Nor have I ever wanted to." She didn't immediately step inside. In spite of all those little windows, it seemed dauntingly black inside the building. "Is there a light in there?"

"Switch is on the wall to your left."

The oddest feeling suddenly assailed her. Anticipation? For two weeks she'd considered nothing but the problems this inheritance represented: the thought of killing animals for pelts generally turned her stomach, and what she was going to do with the place was a growing nightmare. Still, until this moment the minks themselves had never seemed quite real.

Maybe she'd never wanted a fur piece but she was as guilty as the next woman of stroking a stole or coat when she came across one. The craving to touch anything that exquisitely soft was irresistible. Even the thought of mink aroused an instinctive feminine love for anything beautiful, soft, touchable. For the first time in her life she was inches away from being able to stroke the real thing.

"You're sure you want the light on?"

"Of course I'm sure I want the light on."

Still her neighbor blocked the door. His thumbs hooked in his belt loops, he paused. "I honestly think you would be wiser to wait until the morning to do this."

"To see them? Why on earth?"

"Kate—"

"It's Kathryn," she informed him for absolutely the last time, then determinedly ducked inside. Three sets of light fixtures suddenly glared from beneath roof beams. She caught one glimpse of Grant's mouth set in a thin line before all hell broke loose.

Her every sense felt the assault of impressions. Her heart pounded as if she'd been thrown into a nightmare. She saw the shine of two long rows of metal cage upon metal cage. Her nostrils flared because of the unfamiliar smells of raw meat and ammonia and wood chips, but overpowering those scents was a dominantly feral odor, so obnoxious and invasive she could taste it.

Her empty stomach turned inside out in revolt, and her nerves shredded. Maybe she could have handled the smells and sounds, but the instant the lights snapped on, the instant she stepped into the room, the caged creatures hurled and rehurled themselves at their metal doors. She felt surrounded by black beady eyes and wild guttural growls. And their teeth! She could see their tear-you-to-pieces sharp rodents' fangs, all viciously bared, biting at those cages to get out, to get her...

She could no more have stopped herself from backing up than breathing. Two strong arms folded around her shoulders. Never mind what she thought of her neighbor. At that moment she would cheerfully have cuddled up to a friendly gorilla.

"Not exactly amiable little critters, are they? You were expecting tame kittens?"

"I..." As soon as her heart stopped slamming against her chest maybe she'd be able to talk.

"Minks aren't too fond of people, Kate. In fact, I've never run across a more savage breed of animal, and about a third of these had young a month ago. Maternity does nothing to improve their temperament. They let out quite a stink when they're threatened. Almost as bad as a skunk's. Makes some people sick."

Kathryn now knew that. Invisible clouds of the smell were choking her nostrils. She couldn't breathe, and those horrible snarls...

"Look. You're going to be fine. Now just relax. I've got the perfect cure for a little queasy stomach."

The next thing she knew she was sitting on the cement stoop outside the mink shed, feeling mortified and gulping in great quantities of air as fast as her lungs could take it in. She'd had a long day with too much stress and heat, no food, no rest, her damnable headache—she knew exactly why she was overreacting, but that was no excuse for caving in in front of a stranger. Damnation. The earth refused to stop spinning.

Her black-bearded neighbor plucked something from his back pocket before hunkering down next to her. He flipped off the top and firmly wrapped her fingers around the tarnished pint flask.

"Just a sip now. I swear it'll help."

She took more than a sip. She took a good old-fashioned swig and swallowed in one liquid lump. If Kaufman was expecting any ladylike sputters and coughs, he didn't get them. Kathryn had discovered a long time ago that in a predator world, a woman didn't have to like alcohol, but if she wanted to keep that invisible title of lady, she sure as heck had to know how to handle it. At the moment she couldn't be less concerned with titles. To her, possibly the only taste worse than a neat whiskey was Scotch.

As fast as the oily liquid hit her stomach, the nausea faded, her vision cleared and in the background the dreadful sounds of the wretched creatures died down. The only lingering nightmare was the leftover taste on her tongue, which was when it occurred to her that she hadn't just been drinking Scotch. She'd been drinking Chivas Regal.

Men with holey jeans and frayed shirts shouldn't be able to afford that. Or to drink it from sterling—albeit tarnished—silver flasks.

She wasn't about to waste a lot of unnecessary curiosity on an overgrown lumberjack who didn't shave, but her eyes narrowed speculatively on the man sprawled next to her. Something didn't gel. She saw a man who cultivated a wild look with his scraggly beard, a man with dark unruly hair and jeans that would have been rejected by Goodwill. She'd missed the shrewd intelligence in his eyes before and hadn't paid any attention to the character lines drawn with a strong brush on his forehead. Country bumpkins didn't normally have a take-charge presence—or talk with Ivy League accents. Clean him up, put him in a suit, shave off the beard, and . . .

Suddenly she was aware that their thighs were touching. She shifted hers. Promptly. "Thank you," she said belatedly for the drink.

Grant could feel the damn woman trying to jump to conclusions the longer she stared at him. She was the type. Had to poke and pester and analyze everything until it was all notched in neat little boxes. Still, he had to give credit where it was due. "You drink like a man."

She took that as a compliment and figured she'd win even more brownie points if she wiped her mouth on her sleeve, but she wasn't inclined. "Have you lived around here long?" she asked casually.

He stood up slowly and repocketed his flask. "Feeling better?"

So he didn't like personal questions. She could appreciate that. "No, I don't feel better. I feel like an idiot, but darn it, are the minks always that vicious? Is it because they're caged?"

"In the wild they're just as mean. Never open a cage without heavy gloves on. If you fed a starving mink or saved it from sure death, it would still turn on you as fast as it could breathe. They'll attack you with pleasure and not give a damn if you're ten times bigger than they are. They're killers."

"Terrific." So much for visions of darling, cuddly creatures. "Sounds like you know quite a bit about them. You work with animals?"

"I don't work at all." Then he added deliberately, "Never did have much ambition." She was darn good at hiding her expression of distaste, he thought. Even if her eyes registered "You should be ashamed," her voice reeked with tact.

"Well, to each their own. I guess there are times I wish I had less." She stood up and meticulously dusted off the seat of her jeans. Any time now she was going to stop staring at him. He'd clearly established that he was a lackadaisical do-nothing, chalk to her cheese. Heaven knows she had no time for any man in her life right now, and he'd be her last choice if she did.

There was something about him, though. Sexual energy, mystery. She didn't run across many men with shoulders powerful enough to block the sun, eyes so compelling they'd drown a woman's common sense. He emotionally touched her; she felt primitive vibrations. She really wasn't sure whether to be annoyed or amused.

There was no time to be either, she decided. "I noticed a door at the end of the mink shed."

"The feed and slaughtering rooms. I'll show you the rest of your uncle's equipment when I feed the animals in the morning."

She shook her head. "Now would be better really. Then I wouldn't have to bother you again."

He motioned toward the mink shed door. "You're not ready to go back in there."

"Of course I am. I admit I overreacted—"

"Trust me, would you, Kate? Your stomach'll fold flat in half if I show you the slaughtering room."

Her spine straightened, and the spark in her eyes could have lit dynamite fuses. She leveled out a dictatorial, "Look, Mr. Kaufman—"

He really had to grin. He figured she must effectively use that tone on recalcitrant employees. "Honey, you look half dead," he said mildly. "Why don't you just settle in and relax? I'll be back in the morning."

A strand of silk hair had escaped the claw of her hairpins. As fast as he felt the urge to brush it away from her creamy pale cheek, he had the sense to turn away.

That fragile scent of hers could draw in a man. Not him. The dark-lashed blue eyes, the slim white throat—never mind, not him. The woman needed a nap and some food in her stomach. He knew damn well she planned on staying in motion until she crashed. He'd been like that once. He'd run like a mouse in a maze until he'd dropped. He'd forgotten to eat, forgotten to drink and lived on that drive to achieve. She could practice overachieving on her own; he wasn't going to be part of it.

Kathryn couldn't believe her eyes. The darn man had stuffed his hands in his back pockets and was sauntering away. "Wait a minute! I wasn't asking for your help, just a little information. I've only got two weeks here and—Mr. Kaufman—" For a few minutes she'd actually thought he had some potential for membership in the human race. "Mr. Kaufman!" On a last whoosh of breath, she lashed out, "Grant!"

Meek as a lamb, he turned at the sound of his first name. "Now, Kate, I understand you're in a hurry, but I promise to be back in the morning. And I'd help you now, really I would, but I just noticed it was past six. Saturday nights I drink from six to midnight." He shrugged apologetically.

"Well, I certainly wouldn't want to interrupt *that*."

"I knew you wouldn't. I took one look at you and thought, 'Now *there's* a woman who would respect a man's priorities.'"

She caught his arrogant slash of a grin before he turned again. For the first and only time in her life, she wished she were a six-foot-four, two-hundred-and-fifty-pound male with a PhD in wrestling. She'd like to see that unholy smile of his rearranged directly behind his teeth.

In the meantime, she cast a despairing glance in the direction of the cabin. Her mind instantly began prioritizing the catalog of chores required to make the place even nominally sleepable.

Handling Devil-Eyes could wait until tomorrow. It wouldn't take long.

Two
―――

Kathryn slipped off her clogs, draped her towel on the shoulder-high wood partition, and with her hands on her naked hips, viewed the archaic shower contraption. The woods were waking up all around her. Everything green looked as if it were brushed with dew diamonds. A young sun peeked through the tangle of trees in pearl-yellow shafts.

She would have happily sold the sunrise for a chance to get clean. The most civilized part of the shower was the four-sided box, which at least had a wall providing shoulder-to-knee modesty. The rest took logic— and a background in watching westerns—to figure out. One primed the outside pump until it simply wouldn't push anymore, then stepped in, and then, she guessed, simply pulled one of the two dangling chains. She did so.

Three gallons of freezing cold well water obediently gushed on her head, causing her entire body to go into shock and her mouth to utter a long, low series of words, none of them polite. Shaking violently, teeth clenched, she soaped up with Caswell Massey chamomile. Her flesh had barely recovered from the first punishment before she pulled the second chain. Three more gallons of ice water proved an adequate rinse.

Gasping, she grabbed the towel, jammed her bare feet into her clogs and raced for the cabin. Once inside, she bolted for the sleeping loft. The loft was less a room than an open nest—a plump feather mattress cozied up under the bare beams in the corner. Between the bed and her uncle's hand-carved bureau, there was barely room to turn around. Kathryn didn't need space to dress. In two minutes flat she tugged on white cotton jeans and a nubby coral sweater. In two more minutes her damp hair was treated to a French braid, her cheeks to a layer of blush and her eyes to a quick whisk of a mascara wand.

Country living was for the birds . . . a fact she'd already discovered at 5:00 a.m., when an aviary symphony had woken her out of the soundest sleep she'd had in ten years.

Give or take some coffee—preferably acquired soon—she was ready for Grant Kaufman.

She startled a fawn on her brisk walk to the mink shed. Before her neighbor arrived, she hoped to have the minks properly fed and watered. Last night she'd come to the obvious conclusion that her uncle must have had feeding and breeding records somewhere. Once she found them, all she had to do was follow what they said. If and when Kaufman arrived—heaven knows he was probably sleeping off a hangover—she intended to have the job done.

Her step unconsciously slowed as she neared the green-tipped clearing. She found herself staring at the door to the mink shed, not really seeing it. Last night—sometime between washing the kitchen floor and shaking out rugs—she'd built up a fine rage against men in general, and arrogant, lazy men in particular. The force of that rage had disturbed her dreams.

It was still disturbing—the man, yes, but even more, the anger. Lately she seemed to feel perpetually overwound, like a jack-in-the-box always ready to spring up. She used to laugh things off, not let them matter so much. There was a time when she'd had a moment to enjoy a sunrise, time to waste a smile on sunshine. Maybe Grant *was* an overbearing cretin . . . but perhaps she'd been a little quick to judge him. Lately a few too many people had suggested she was a little on the abrupt, domineering side herself.

She never used to be like that. She never used to be angry, impatient, insensitive to people. It wasn't how she wanted to be; it was just that the pressure never let up. Life never stopped pushing. The treadmill never slowed down. As fast as she handled one problem, another jumped into its place.

At the moment there was a problem standing in front of her. Lips firmly shut in determination, she pushed open the shed door. Deliberately not turning on the light, she stepped into the gloomy darkness and braced herself. As soon as they sensed her presence, the minks rustled warily in their cages, but there were no instant snarls, none of that repulsive odor they'd sprayed yesterday.

"That's right, easy now," she murmured. "Believe me, I don't like strangers any more than you do. No one's going to hurt you. All I want to do is feed you and give you some nice fresh water. Easy now..."

Crooning nonsense, she took a moment to let her eyes adjust to the dimness. The windows let in shaded daylight, but no direct sun. At the end of the long room was a door; she assumed it led to the feed area Grant had mentioned. Getting there was the problem. Tiptoeing the gauntlet of shiny, beady eyes, she passed between the rows of cages. "Easy now..."

Her palms were damp, her pulse racing. Both exasperated her. She'd either been too shook up or too tired to really see the animals yesterday. Now she could make out the incomparable sheen and luxurious softness of their fur. The gleam of an especially silvery pelt drew her an inch closer to one cage.

The mink bared his teeth and let out a low warning growl that set her nerves jangling. "Now, calm down..." A second mink picked up the signal. Animal teeth gnashed together.

Swallowing hard, Kathryn perched her hands on her hips. If her voice was still a Crosby croon, there was a trace of steel in it. "Now, look, you guys. This is ridiculous. You think you're real scary, don't you? Well, if you want to know about intimidating, I'll tell you about intimidating. Growing up on the south side of Chicago—*that's* intimidating. Never having enough to eat, left alone as a kid because your mom had to work at night, being evicted when there wasn't enough for rent...I know all about being scared witless, you little monsters, and believe me you're pipsqueaks by comparison. I've handled tougher than you with both hands tied behind my back. Now darn it, *stop* that!"

They did. In fact, the creatures quieted down so obediently that Kathryn frowned. Then a sixth sense made her whirl toward the shadow in the doorway.

Heat rolled through her veins when she recognized Grant. One of his worn leather boots was set forward. His shoulder leaned negligently against the doorjamb as if he'd been relaxed in that position for some time. "Good morning, Kate."

She'd promised herself to stay patient if and when she ran into him again. She didn't know the man from Adam; he wasn't worth anger or frustration. It took two to clash, and if she maintained a cool, friendly attitude, he'd never have another chance to rub her the wrong way.

His husky greeting instantly rubbed her wrong. So did the slow male speculation in his eyes. He'd overheard her talking to herself. She must have sounded like an idiot, but it wasn't embarrassment that stirred an annoying sensation of nervousness. Casual friendliness and Grant just weren't going to go together.

He was too big, too rough, too wild-looking. Male predators roamed asphalt streets as well as north country woods. Kathryn had met her share, but there was no question that he was different. His hair was thick, untamed and as black as a panther's coat. His forearm muscles were honed so smoothly you could see the pulse of veins inside, and the sheer force of the man made her feel small, fragile, unsure. Those sensations distressed her. Any woman at thirty-one had learned to be a judge of men. Why was it so hard to fathom this one?

"You're up early," he said quietly.

"Yes." Her gaze tipped to the second shadow in the doorway, waist-high and massive. "Good heavens, what's that?"

"Baby—stay!" he ordered the dog.

The minks went crazy. Kathryn ignored them and him, hopelessly charmed by his "Baby." With the single command from Grant, the dog dropped to the ground outside. Her drooping red eyes registered helpless despair. Her jowls sagged, and her forehead was a mass of wrinkles. She looked like a worried hundred-and-ten-year-old woman.

"She is a bloodhound, isn't she?" Kathryn couldn't help but move forward to pet the dog.

"She's a total klutz who'll bay all night at a full moon. Worthless, greedy, clumsy, lazy..." Since his eyes rested on the dog with pure affection, his words didn't carry much weight. When he glanced back at Kathryn, she felt his dark eyes skim her long legs, breasts, throat, mouth...lightning streaked through a peaceful, sunny morning. Challenges were issued. Nothing complicated, just pure sexual voltage strong enough to make her toes curl.

Kathryn informed herself that a little tingle of lust was justifiable, but not for the man. She'd just noticed the thermos tucked under his arm. It had to hold coffee.

For caffeine she could manage casual friendliness if it killed her. "You had a good time last night?" she asked cheerfully.

"Last night?"

"You drink on Saturdays. Remember?" She wouldn't think he had to be reminded.

"I remember." He straightened. "I also remember that on Sunday mornings we feed the minks. Ready?"

Suddenly all business—for which she was grateful—he strode toward the far end of the mink shed. Ducking through a narrow doorway, he switched on an overhead fluorescent light. The concrete floors and walls were painted white, and contrary to absolutely everything she'd seen since she'd come here, the room was spotless.

"The feed room," Grant said shortly, and motioned to the equipment. "Hogger, mixer, grinder and refrigerator units. It may not look like much, but your uncle has better than a sixty-thousand-dollar investment in here."

"So I understand from the papers the lawyer left me. It's hard to believe, considering the shape of the cabin."

"He gave the animals the best, no question of that. There's food ahead in that freezer unit for at least a month. He also had the best of modern cages. By using a pullout feed system, there was rarely need to handle the animals at all."

"That sounds kind of cruel. Maybe if they'd been handled, they wouldn't be so mean."

Grant shook his head, moving toward the giant refrigerator. "Two minks come together and they'll tear each other apart. If you touch a mother's young kit, she'll eat the little one. Pure and simple—they don't care for contact, human or any other."

It seemed ironic that humans could never resist the soft fur of the one animal who hated touch. Kathryn was about to comment on the strange vagaries of nature but then didn't. Grant wasn't exactly inviting casual conversation. "All right. So what do they eat?"

That was more complicated than she imagined. Their diet varied according to season. In winter, when the animals were already of a size and had their prime coat, they were fed a maintenance diet—mostly raw fish with a light mix of raw meat and fortified cereals. In spring, the minks were bred, and those females then required raw liver and strong-muscled red meats. Fall was the season when the animals grew their winter pelt—their good fur—and at that point diet was the most critical thing of all.

"But that's what you'd feed them if you were a fur grower," Kathryn finally said impatiently. "What do they actually *like* to eat?"

"You mean in the wild?" He'd moved to the white Formica counter and was unwrapping presized packages.

"Yes."

"Really, about the same thing. They're flesh eaters, part of the same weasel family as ferrets and skunks. They generally live near water. They'll prey on frogs, bugs, snakes, an occasional small bird, all the small mammals— Kate, what on earth are you doing?"

She glanced up from the pen and small pad of paper in her hand. "Taking notes." Glancing at his expression, she immediately shoved the pad into her back pocket. "I'm sorry. I should be helping you, shouldn't I? I'll be glad to do it all, for heaven's sake— it was just that you were so busy. I was trying to stay out of your way and just watch so I'd know the next time . . ."

Taking notes. Grant shook his head. A priceless summer morning with woods full of wildflowers and a sun heating up an entire sky, and she was taking notes.

He'd stalked over here in a frame of mind bad enough to bite off anyone's head who'd crossed his path. A sleepless night had produced that general mood, and the blonde in front of him was the direct source of his insomnia. He'd had every intention of tending to the minks before she'd risen. But he should have known better. The Kathryns of this life didn't sleep. They ran in circles, achieving, striving, accomplishing. They raced past sunsets, past the gurgle of a child's laughter, past the sound of silence on a cold winter night. They missed life while they were taking all those notes.

As that thought occurred to him, he knew he'd prejudged her, maybe unfairly, and that he was still doing it. He also knew why. It had to do with the white column of her throat above the V of her coral sweater, with hair the color of sunlight and with that soft, soft skin. At thirty-five Grant knew damn well when he was attracted to a woman.

But he didn't want to be attracted to this one. With a nag of irritation he could see that she looked just as tired now as the night before. She moved with the same frenetic restlessness, the same need to constantly do; her hands didn't know how to stay still.

Grant was a rational man, and his head warned him to stay clear. His dreams the night before had been distinctly irrational. He'd dreamed about that intense, vibrant energy of hers. He'd dreamed about all that passion released in a man's bed—his. He'd dreamed about taking the pins out of her hair, feeling her restless hands on him... He hadn't let a fantasy go like that since he was a teenage boy.

"Like this?"

He erased the scowl from his forehead and glanced where she was pulling out the cage drawer to drop in the premeasured food. "Exactly."

They were half finished feeding the minks when he let an ounce—no more—of curiosity escape him. "So. You grew up in Chicago?"

"Born and bred."

"South side?"

She smiled at him. Like the tease of treasure, he was suddenly distracted. Her lips curled with the faintest slash of coral when she smiled. "We need nose plugs in this place."

"The smell of raw meat's a long way from perfume," he agreed, and decided he wasn't going to ask her anything else.

That worked for a time, except that once she got the hang of the feed and watering technique, she took to it like a pro, maintaining his pace and then exceeding it. Even watching her was exhausting. "You sleep all right in the cabin?"

"Sure."

"You probably have the whole day planned." He knew that answer even before she replied with a light chuckle. Almost as if she were talking to herself, she listed her schedule.

"I only quit cleaning last night when I ran out of soap. I brought some supplies with me, but I'll have to go into town to get more. Soap, food . . . the place *has* to have curtains . . . I'll need some tools for the yard. And I have to call home— I own a store in Chicago. First and foremost, though, I'm hoping to find someone who might be a potential buyer for the ranch." She stopped. "You're not interested, are you? I should have asked you yesterday. You obviously know a lot about this—"

"No way. Any place with livestock, you're tied down day in, day out."

"Not your style?" she murmured dryly.

"Not my style," he confirmed. "Kate?"

"Hmm?"

"Are you going to pour yourself a cup of coffee or just keep staring at that thermos? I didn't bring it over here for me. And when we're done here, I'll take a look at that stove up at the cabin. If you haven't run a woodburner before, it might give you some trouble."

"Thank you," she said carefully. He appeared terrified she was going to accuse him of thoughtfulness.

At the cabin, he did more than show her how to work the cookstove. He chopped a stack of kindling, taught her how to fill and prime the wick on the kerosene lanterns, then did something or other with the water pump to make it push easier.

Grant had no intention of getting involved, but the darn woman was a walking cyclone. She picked up an ax like she was dying to lose a finger. He had visions of forest fires the way she handled the lanterns, and once he got the stove going she had eggs in a skillet before he could stop her. He figured that the only way she'd eat was if he stayed for breakfast himself.

That was a mistake in judgment on his part. She didn't eat, but, with his chin in his palm and a mug of coffee in his other hand, he watched her try. Toby's wallpaper was what did her in.

He'd first caught her glancing at it when she'd fumbled in a drawer for silverware. While the eggs had fried, he'd watched her flick a thumbnail where the paper was peeling the most. She'd immediately washed her hands, but when she'd set the table her gaze had zipped back up to the wall. At the moment, with her completely forgotten plate of eggs in one hand, she'd already peeled off one strip and was working on another.

"Sit down, Kate," he said patiently.

"This'll come off like nothing. I won't even need a solvent!"

He wondered vaguely when a man had excited her this much. "You don't think it'll wait two minutes until you've had something to eat?"

"I am eating. And you were just about to tell me how long you've lived around here."

"Five years, give or take."

"Then you're not originally from the area?"

She not only incessantly moved; she incessantly asked questions. "You had a store, you said."

"Women's clothing," she said absently. "I started out with a little boutique, but cute little boutiques don't make it. Women browse in places like that, but they don't buy."

"So... what do they buy?"

"Heaven knows, but I'll tell you what a woman wants in a clothing store these days. A place she can zip in and zip out, where she can find what she wants in seconds. A place that sells cashmere and pearls at dime-store prices. A place that makes her feel virtuous because she's being practical, and wicked at the same time because she can't resist the clothes." She added humorously, "That overall package isn't always easy to provide."

"Do pretty well at it?"

"This year I'm out of the red. It was a long time coming." The cracked wall beneath the paper was a putrid yellow. She wrinkled her nose at it. "I suppose I'll need putty or something like that for the cracks." She glanced at Grant.

"What you need is to leave it for the new owner, since you sound pretty sure you want to sell the place. Let him tackle the mess."

She shook her head. The longer she talked to Grant, the more it became obvious he was a leave-it-for-tomorrow type—her diametric opposite in every way. "I can't stand leaving things," she said frankly. "Never could."

"You're not going to stand at all unless you occasionally give your body a little sustenance. There are two eggs still sitting on that plate."

"I'll get to them."

Maybe by midnight. Grant watched her push the kitchen chair over to the wall and stand on it. When she lifted an arm, her coral sweater separated from her jeans. Just an inch. An inch of pearl-white abdomen. "You always lived in Chicago?" he asked.

"Yup. Grew up on the wrong side of the tracks." Her tone was as light as a breeze. "Most of the girls in fifth grade carried switchblades. It was that kind of neighborhood. My worst nightmares used to be about oatmeal."

"Oatmeal?"

"There were days we had oatmeal for breakfast, lunch and dinner." Her voice was still light, all sassy humor. Only someone listening closely would have heard the trace of old fears in her voice, old anxieties, old memories. "There was just my mom and me. She worked like a dog, cleaning other people's houses. When I was ten years old, I knew I was going to get her out of there."

"And you did," he said quietly.

That gentle tenor touched something in Kathryn she didn't want touched. Her depth of loss and love for her mother was a private thing. She whisked past the emotions, spilling the words like careless trinkets. "Yes, I got her out. Not soon enough. She died three years ago." Rapidly she jumped down from the chair and started to thread through the overflowing drawer next to the back door. Her uncle seemed to have saved everything from bottle caps to shoelaces. All she wanted was a scraper. "I was married once. Did I tell you that?"

"No."

"Well, I was. Two years, thankfully long over now. The failure was mine, not John's. He was a good man, very gentle. All he wanted was a wife—not a part-time lover already married to a store. I seem to have this gift of failing the people who really matter to me until it's too late. And there's really an excellent reason why I'm spilling all this personal nonsense that's absolutely none of your business, Kaufman."

"Oh?" He didn't mean to, but when she waved the screwdriver at him like a teacher's pointer, he couldn't help grinning.

"Yes. You're not getting out of here scot-free. It'll be your turn to talk after this."

"Kate, you can't use a screwdriver to peel off wall-paper."

"Certainly I can." She saw that he had a wonder-ful smile, winsome and boyish and sexy. Laughter jumped in his eyes when he relaxed and forgot all about scowling.

At some point when they'd been feeding the minks, she'd accepted that her curiosity about him wasn't going to go away. She had been wrong about him. Al-though Grant looked the part of a bearded vagrant, he moved like lightning when he chose, took charge with natural familiarity, and whether he knew it or not, as-sumed responsibility as if it were second nature. He also held on to his secrets like a toddler with a fistful of candy. If Kathryn wanted a few answers from him, she figured she'd have to cough up some of her own first.

It wasn't such a terrible price. At most she was going to be here two weeks, and then she'd never see him again. What difference did it make what he knew about her? "You must live pretty close by if you walk over here," she started probing.

"A half mile or so through the woods."

"And you're originally from where?"

"Gary."

"Indiana?" The industrial town was just outside of Chicago.

"Yes, Indiana." He stood up to rinse his plate. He couldn't continue to sit there and watch her spin through energy like a spider in the rain. If he stayed any longer, he knew he'd be drawn in to scraping wallpaper . . . and answering questions he didn't want to answer. "I'll be back at five to feed the minks."

She set the screwdriver on the table, then dusted her hands on her jeans. Soft color brushed her cheeks. She'd meant no harm with her curiosity. A quick, innocuous sharing of life histories hadn't struck her as prying, but maybe it did to him. "You don't have to come back, Grant. Honestly, I think I can manage the animals from here. You've done more than enough as it is."

He hadn't done enough, he realized, the instant he saw her face tilted up to his. Her blue eyes were disarmingly shaded by velvet lashes, and three wisps of champagne hair floated on her forehead.

He hadn't come back to hear her life story. He already knew that drive, anger and fear made up ambition; he'd already guessed that Kathryn had learned about all of those too young. He hadn't come back to feel the fierce pull of compassion and caring for a sprite of a woman who'd had to fight too many battles alone, and he certainly hadn't come back to fix her stove. He'd come back to find out if there was a chance in hell she ever stood still.

She stood motionless when his palm cupped her face. He could feel her tense with wariness, see the shock of surprise in her eyes at that first contact. He saw the pulse working in her throat and knew darn well that white throat was filling up with words to reject the pass. Kathryn, he guessed, had rejected a lot of passes in her time. Tactfully of course. Without question, she'd be polite. Firm. Efficient in putting a man off.

She saw those brooding dark eyes coming toward her and could have cursed herself for letting down her guard. Where she came from, a little casual conversation wasn't an invitation. Never mind. Once he discovered what it was like to kiss a chip of ice, he'd back off.

She stood patiently, mentally counting all the things she had to do as soon as he left, while his palm cradled her cheek, forcing her face closer. All right, you're curious, Kaufman? she thought. So get it over with. I've got better things to do than get in a fistfight with you. His fingers slid into her hair, loosening the French braid she'd put in that morning. A nuisance, having to redo that when he left. Her eyes met his, brimming with amusement. Don't you think this is a little silly? she thought. We're grown-ups, Grant. Old enough to know that even a casual encounter is just plain foolishness. You don't seriously want this any more than I do.

The smallest frown gradually creased her brow. He'd stopped moving forward. The walls blurred behind him; sunlight softened in the distant window. Grant filled her focus with sharp, distinct clarity. She saw an unsmiling mouth buried in that wild beard of his. She saw eyes fastened with satin intensity on her face. He was simply waiting, and from nowhere she felt the oddest shiver of fear.

Exactly then, when air was locked in her lungs, his mouth covered hers. Like the rush of a wave the kiss kept coming, building up tension, power and momentum with evocative speed. His beard was rough, ticklish and disturbing in texture next to the softness of his lips. He teased her with that softness, and then he claimed her mouth with a pressure that forced her heart to flutter like a trapped bird.

She'd been kissed her share before. She'd received iced tea flavored kisses and whiskey flavored kisses, pecks and smooches and skilled invitations-to-bed kisses, but never one like this. He took. He tasted like coffee, and his hands kept lazily threading through her hair. She could feel the brace of his thighs against hers, the sexual heat of him.

When she stood still as a statue, he lifted his lips from hers. Brooding eyes touched her mouth, her hair, her eyes...and she saw challenge in his slow smile before he began his second assault. This time he wrapped her in long, strong arms. He surrounded her. Her instincts announced her tactical error. Before, he might have settled for a token response; now he was determined to achieve a total meltdown.

When the sky turned red, she wanted to tell him. And if he had given her a second to breathe, to think, to logically worry about all this, she probably would have. Kisses weren't like this. Especially first kisses. First kisses were sugary, not a lazy, dark, sensual immersion of the senses. Not gravity falling, not this silly spinning...damn the man!

There was no place for her hands to go but on his shoulders, and the instant she touched him she heard his husky sound of approval. His mouth sealed hers possessively, and slowly his hands slid intimately down her spine. Somewhere far away a curtain fluttered in a sunlit breeze. Much closer was a man's arousal pressed intimately against her, a hunger far too raw for this early in the morning and kisses that exhalted in the difference between man and woman in the most primitive way.

It wasn't that she didn't know better than to respond. She just hadn't expected the flash of silver under her closed eyelids. Something delicious and lazy curled inside her, like the tease of a promise, something she hadn't guessed at, hadn't known before. Something wild, like a storm at sunrise. Something soft, like the wash of a rainbow. Something frightening that kept drawing her down and in, deeper, where it was dark and hot, too hot . . .

Grant sensed the bewilderment that colored her desire. Her breath was as sweet as it was quick and uneven. Her fingers were all but unraveling the shoulder of his shirt. Yes, he wanted all of that. He wanted every feeling he could arouse in her—nerves, need, tension, wanting. Even fear, if she felt fear.

A kiss was feeling, nothing more, but it should be nothing less. He'd be damned if she'd think about real estate appointments and minks or her Chicago store at the same time. Emotion was all he wanted to communicate to her, all he wanted from her. Life was hard. Did she think he didn't understand? But it was harder if you let yourself lose that capacity to feel, let be, let happen, touch.

He had intended a simple lesson; he hadn't bargained on feeling the return lance of an emotional ricochet. Kate was precious. When her lips yielded, when she gave in and her long, lithe body went soft, he felt sanity slipping. Her hair felt too much like silk, the taste of her too much like a drug. She could shatter a man with potential alone. So much heat and warmth, need and softness lurked just beneath the surface.

Why couldn't she have been ice?

Kathryn rocked back the instant she felt him pull away. A beam of sunlight lanced his grave features and dark eyes. Was he angry? Surely she was the one who should be angry. And maybe she would be in a moment, but not now, not yet. She felt disoriented, as if she'd stepped into a scene on a stage where she couldn't possibly belong. Obviously some other woman had been in the bearded stranger's arms. It couldn't have been her.

But it was *her* cheeks that felt the intimate burn of his beard, her lips the bruising tenderness of his. Her whole body felt hot, embarrassingly aroused, shaken by his touch. "I..." Her tongue felt thick. She couldn't think of a thing to say.

"Fun, wasn't it?"

"Fun?" Something fragile and special abruptly took on the color of hurt.

"But not to worry, Kate. It would be like Jekyll and Hyde having an affair— I can't think of anything worse." He shoved his hands in his back pockets as he headed for the door. "Relax. Believe me, that won't happen again. And dammit, eat those eggs. I'll be back at five for the minks."

"Kaufman!"

But he was gone.

Three

———

Kathryn climbed out of the car, pushed her sunglasses to the top of her head and viewed the derelict restaurant with an exasperated sigh. A three o'clock Sunday sun blazed down on the place just ahead, reflecting peeling green paint on a screen door with rusty hinges. The gravel parking lot was bordered with weeds, and a hand-painted sign advertised a special on catfish.

A bad day showed no sign of getting better. Swinging the straps of her purse to her shoulder, she strode toward the creaking door. Predictably it banged behind her.

It took a few seconds for her eyes to adjust to the dim interior, but she didn't have to blink twice to realize there were only men in the place—maybe a dozen of them—all of whom stopped their conversations to witness her entrance. The word "restaurant" was clearly an excuse to keep a bar open on a Sunday afternoon. Two pool tables were in use at the far end of the room. To her right, somewhere beneath clouds of cigar smoke, a poker game was in progress. She could smell beer, smoke, peanuts and men's sweat in varying proportions. She was a long way from the Ritz.

"Hi, darlin'."

She moved past the whiskered gent with the too-friendly smile and ignored the wolf whistle from the poker table. Men weren't on her good list to begin with today, but at least, for the first time since eight that morning, her mind was completely distracted from Grant.

The bartender was leaning on his elbows at the bar, making no pretense of doing anything but watching her approach. Bald, except for a wispy fluff of hair, his voice had a boom that undoubtedly echoed in Canada. "Well, now, what can I do for you, little lady?"

"You're Petey?"

"Sure am, darlin'."

"I was just at the fishing tackle store. The owner— Jeannie Watson?—said you might help me find a man named Bud Spenser."

"Sure will." Fluff directed his boom toward the poker table. "Bud! Get over here! The little lady's looking for you." His tone gentled to a sheepish apology. "Pardon my tone, Miss."

"Just tell her to come over here!"

From the distance of table to bar, it was hardly necessary to shout. Failing to find a nice hole to crawl in, Kathryn, a fixed smile on her face, maneuvered around tables toward the poker group. Immediately five men pushed back their chairs and hustled to shove a rickety stool up to the table for her. "Sit down there, honey."

"Yeah, sit down here."

When the first wave of cigar smoke cleared, she found a dripping beer stein and a nearly empty bowl of peanuts placed in front of her. Beer bellies bulged over belts. All these good ole boys were of an age where their whiskers showed gray and their hair was thinning. Four looked friendly. The fifth obviously held a winning poker hand and didn't appreciate the interruption.

"Help yourself, help yourself. What can I do for you, sweetheart?" Bud Spenser asked.

"I'm terribly sorry to interrupt your poker game." More than they knew. "I was simply trying to locate a Mr. Spenser."

"I'm Bud, sweetie. Nobody here'd know who you were talking about if you use that Mr. Spenser business. You have to be Toby Price's niece."

"Yes."

"You guys playing or planning on chitchatting all afternoon? Freda's going to fry my butt as it is, sitting here when there's a yard to get mowed," said the man with the winning hand.

"Shut up, Baker. Give the lady a chance to say her piece. You'll get her all shook up with your bad manners." The man named Spenser had a hawk's beak and a wild head of iron-red hair. He grinned at her. "Now you just go ahead, Miss."

Heat climbed her cheeks. She never could stand being the center of attention, and that's exactly what she'd been all morning. As she went from the fishing tackle store to the gas station to the corner grocery, the sleepy little northern town had tumbled over itself trying to help her. Apart from all the supplies she'd had to buy, the back of her car now held a borrowed push lawn mower and a donated pair of rusty clippers. Not that she wasn't grateful, but the only help she needed was to find someone—*anyone*—who had either the desire or equity to take on a mink ranch.

So far, everywhere she turned, she was directed to Grant Kaufman. She wasn't allowed to erase the man from her mind. No one in town handled real estate, but she could ask Grant. The closest vet was an hour and a half's drive, but she could ask Grant. Sure, there were mink ranches peppered throughout the Upper Peninsula, but no one knew exactly where. She could ask Grant. He might know.

She was not in a mood to ask Grant anything after this morning, and she could make no sense of the town's fascination with her neighbor. She'd heard his story, from gray-haired Jeanne Watson at the tackle store to the dark-haired nymph at the gas station and every other woman in town.

The girls all figured Grant had a dark romantic past. He'd shown up five years before and had simply stayed, keeping to himself, living off the land pioneer style. He was wonderful with animals; he'd patched up every kid's pet for a twenty-mile radius. And his Baby was famous—the bloodhound had tracked more than one city tourist who'd gotten lost somewhere between the imagination and reality of camping in wilderness country. As far as Grant, though, the females in town had done their best to rouse him out of hibernation. The poor darling had to be lonely. They figured all he needed was a good woman.

The more Kathryn listened, the more she figured that what he needed was a good kick in the seat of his pants. She'd never been much impressed by dark romantic pasts. Obviously the man had no visible means of support and never worked if he didn't have to.

Seven hours before, she'd been wrapped around that total derelict like a candy wrapper over chocolate. The memory of that embrace was still upsetting her. At the moment she was tired of the man, his name and her own curiosity about him. When Jeannie Watson told her that Bud Spenser was a former mink rancher, Kathryn had jumped at the lead. Would he possibly be interested in buying or managing the property?

"Well, now…" Bud stroked his whiskered chin. "I really can't help you there, Miss Price. I got out of that business sometime back, and good riddance. The risk was too high for all the trouble the varmints were worth." He turned to the rest. "Anybody got any idea for her?"

A codger missing a front tooth suggested, "You know a man named Grant Kaufman?"

"Yes." She resisted the urge to grit her teeth. "I've met him."

"Well, he's probably the best one to ask. Knows everybody around that's into any kind of animals. See, we don't have any vet close by. He's patched up every kid's—"

"Yes." She'd already heard. "Mr., Bud," she corrected quickly. "The thing is that I have a business in Chicago. The absolute longest I can stay here is two weeks. I'm not worried so much about the cabin or property because they can both wait, but the animals can't. I have to find someone to take them on. If you misunderstood—I'm not asking for money. I'd be delighted to give them to someone free and clear. Surely someone..."

None of the five knew of anyone.

"Look, if you want them slaughtered, I'll do it for you," a man named Reefer offered.

"No," Kathryn said instantly, and then bit her lip in frustration. She hadn't meant to sound unfriendly, but that offer had already been made to her once. It had turned her stomach then and it turned it now.

"You need to see Grant," Bud repeated.

"Yup, you ask Kaufman," Reefer affirmed. "Still, if you get in a bind, little lady, don't forget my offer. I don't know nothing about the pelt business, but I got a good shotgun."

"She don't want you to do that, Reefer, can't you see that? And besides, that'd be all that investment down the drain. Toby had a fortune in the place. Heard there's more than one mink ranch west of here, Newberry and McMillan way."

"Far from here?" Kathryn asked quickly.

"An hour's drive, or so. Can't say as I know anybody you could ask direct."

"Grant might know."

"Yeah, Kaufman'd know if anybody would."

Swell. A half hour later, Kathryn stood outside an open phone booth near the gas station, poking coin after coin into the slots. Her cotton sweater was sticking to her under a broiling sun. Passing cars kicked up grit in the dustbowl road, and her throat was parched. Her palm brushed the sticky tendrils at her nape as she waited for Bess to answer.

When the Chicago connection was finally made, her assistant sounded breathless. Kathryn could easily picture her. Young and pretty, Bess had a degree in retailing, and the drive and determination to talk Kathryn into a partnership—preferably yesterday. Bess was capable. It was the "young" that had Kathryn worried about leaving her assistant alone with the shop for too long. "So they arrived damaged? Bess, in the top drawer of my desk there's the telephone number for—"

"Kathryn, I know, and I've already called them. Would you please stop worrying? Everything's going fine. We had a flood of customers yesterday!"

"You were busy. I should have been there." Kathryn rubbed two fingers on her temples.

"You should *not* be here. You haven't taken two hours off since I've known you. What you *should* be doing is enjoying a little sunshine, a little vacation for a change. For heaven's sake, Kathryn, relax. I can handle this." Her voice took on a humorous note. "Find any good-looking rugged men up there?"

All Kathryn had found was a lazy renegade who stole kisses with dangerous skill, something she wasn't inclined to mention to Bess. "I'm not up here looking for men," she reminded her assistant irritably.

"Somehow I had high hopes you'd find a nice backwoods mellow type you could lie out in the sun with."

Kathryn stared at the receiver. "Have I ever struck you as the type to lie out in the sun?"

"It wouldn't kill you. And every woman needs a little affair once in a while."

"Could we move this discussion back to the store?" Kathryn demanded crisply. "There are two other calls I forgot to ask you to make..."

Fifteen minutes later the sun hadn't gotten any cooler, and discouragement was nagging her usually high energy level. Chicago seemed to be surviving reasonably well without her. The problem was, she didn't seem to be surviving at all without Chicago.

Every road she turned down in this backwater wilderness proved to be a dead end.

Even worse, all roads seemed to lead back to Grant Kaufman.

* * *

The last time Grant had worn a white shirt was for a funeral. The starched collar was driving him nuts now. His hair was still damp from a shower, and the wicker basket in his arm held three wrapped, almost thawed steaks and a bottle of '83 Coron. The bloodhound at his side had had a bath.

Altogether it was a lot of trouble for a man to go through to apologize to a woman he wasn't even interested in, but he seemed to be stuck with a nagging conscience. He'd given Kathryn a pretty hard time since she'd arrived, all because the lady happened to remind him of a world he wanted left behind. A grown man didn't hang his emotional laundry in front of a woman, and he also didn't take advantage of one when she was vulnerable.

All day long he hadn't been able to forget the look in her eyes when he'd left that morning. She was shook and she was mad and she was hurt...and it was his fault. All he'd meant was to force her to loosen up a little, enjoy, feel, relax. There was more to life than infernal busyness. It had taken him many years to realize that, but when it came down to it, what possible business was it of his if Kate chose to take that same dead-end road?

None.

What right did he have to interfere in her life?

None.

What right did he have to attack her like a steamroller in her own kitchen, or slough off a woman's exquisitely fragile response with a blithe putdown?

None.

Lord, the guilt. And the collar was killing him. Grimacing, he threaded a finger between the starched linen and his neck as he opened the door of the mink shed. One glance told him the minks were all freshly fed and watered. It was going on six.

More guilt. He'd told her he'd take care of the minks at five. Heaven knows, she was the type to consider a time schedule sacred. "Come on, Baby." The bloodhound seemed inclined to take the day's fiftieth nap under the shed's maple tree. "I hope you've planned what to say to her, because I sure as hell haven't."

He was worked up to a dark frazzle by the time he emerged from the woods by the cabin. Signs of her trip to town were everywhere. A lawn mower sat smothered in weeds, and a tray of pansies sat on the step, waiting to be planted. The porch was swept, and a brand-new welcome mat was sitting in front of the door. Windows gleamed. In fact, the windows moved. Frowning, he cocked his head to see as he mounted the porch steps. She had to be standing on a chair. He could see her from breast to waist, and she was holding something white and frothy in her hands. Curtains, he recognized belatedly.

Trust Kate to be still working when she'd been up at five and in town half the day. He dropped the basket outside and rapped once on the door, then poked his head inside before he could completely change his mind about visiting.

"Well, hi, Grant."

Over the top of a curtain rod, her blue eyes appeared serene and calm. Her lips curled in a casual smile.

He hadn't expected a friendly reception. "Hi," he said firmly, and then cleared his throat. "Listen, Kate—"

"Right there—could you hand me those scissors?"

"Where? Oh…" He grabbed them off the floor and lifted them up to her. "Listen, I brought some steaks, and I thought—"

"And that little box of pins?"

"Pins?"

"Right there on the table."

He handed her those, too, and then pushed a hand through his hair. "Could you listen for a minute?"

"Sure."

But the whole place distracted him. Everything smelled like lemon oil instead of dust. Toby's couch was saddle leather; he'd always thought it was brown. A roll of wallpaper sat on the kitchen table, feminine stuff, with a copper pot and leaf pattern. And Kathryn herself looked fresh and smelled like some kind of flower. His gaze was at eye level to her fanny. "KATHRYN," he said irritably.

She mumbled something blithe through a mouthful of pins.

"It's time to eat. I brought over some steaks. I figured I'd cook them over a fire if you were hungry. If you're not hungry, fine." As fast as the words were out, he could have kicked himself. That wasn't what he'd intended to say at all.

She pushed the last pin into the curtain hem. "That sounds fine," she said cheerfully. "Just give me a minute to put all this away."

"I thought I'd build a fire—"

"Yes, I heard you."

"I'm not saying I blame you for being irritated, but I figured by now you were hungry. And maybe if we—"

"Why on earth would I be irritated? I think your idea's terrific, and very honestly, I'm starved."

"Well . . . fine." He was tempted to shake her. Obviously she hadn't spent a second's worry on an embrace that had torn him apart all day.

"I like that white shirt."

He glared at her. For five fantastic years he'd cultivated peace. One look at that demure smile and he felt threatened by something sticky and dangerous. Civilized female trickery. The confounded woman wasn't going to give him the chance to make a clean apology, which left him nowhere to get rid of the guilt. Everything was going wrong, and he hadn't been this nervous since he'd picked up his date for the junior prom. It had to be Kathryn's fault.

"Something wrong, Grant?"

"Everything's fine," he enunciated clearly. Or it would be fine, once he got her out in his woods, calmed her down with a perfectly flamed steak and softened her up with a little wine. His plan only had one small flaw. He was the one who wasn't calm and who needed the wine most.

Kathryn noticed that. It suited her purpose to have Grant off-balance. He deserved to suffer a little guilt over his treatment of her this morning. Between her phone call to Chicago and return to the cabin, she'd had ample time to think. From the humorous side of the fence, a woman did what a woman had to do. Since no one else had been considerate enough to teach the wild beast manners, the buck might as well stop with her.

And from the serious side of the fence—whether she liked it or not, whether she wanted it or not, whether she could live with it or not—she was stuck needing the man.

She didn't complain once about the swarms of blackflies en route to his picnic site, and she didn't suggest that it would take far less time and trouble to cook the steaks near the cabin.

"Now, I know this isn't exactly the Holiday Inn...."

"It's delightful, Grant. Really."

He shot her another disbelieving glance. She smiled, then poured wine for both of them. He'd brought glasses—a miracle. The 1983 Coron raised yet another question in her mind concerning her neighbor's mysterious character—wine like that was sure as heck not sold in these parts, nor was it inexpensive. But for the moment she put all those considerations aside, not because she wanted to, but because that first sip of dry, fine wine hit her like a submarine.

Darn it, she was tired. Itchy tired, restless tired, months-of-too-much-pressure tired. The wine soothed her throat like languid honey. Grant had stretched out the cotton blanket in a space between two trees. Just beside her was a narrow creek spinning a winding silver path over rocks and stones. The sun had turned a mellow orange and was cradled in the treetops, and his woods were the kind where all the trees were huge and gnarled and old. It was so cool. She'd been so hot all day. Everything was green and black and silver, and then there was a flare of yellow when Grant lit a match to the crisscross bed of kindling he'd assembled.

She thought absently that he looked like an Indian. His white shirt only accented his bronze skin and powerful shoulders. He moved lithely around the fire, at once at ease in the natural environment and yet always aware. She didn't doubt that he would have thrived here a hundred years before, nor did she think he'd ever need telephones and refrigerators to survive. The wild country suited him. She couldn't imagine him needing anyone but himself.

His eyes met hers over the fire, and she found herself staring, disturbingly aware of exactly why she'd blindly responded to him that morning. Grant was self-reliant, independent, content inside himself, as wild and free as the woods, the air. He was what she wanted to be. To touch him was to reach out for what she desperately wanted.

The harder she fought for security, the fiercer the battle to attain and achieve, the tighter she could feel the ropes of pressure and responsibility. There were days she'd have sold her soul for someone to hold on to. Not help her, not talk, not work, just ... hold.

"Kate?"

He was still staring at her over the fire. She swallowed another sip of wine. "Hmm?"

"I'm sorry. I was out of line this morning."

"It's all right." An apology was more than she'd expected, and suddenly the game of keeping him off-balance seemed petty. "Grant, I need your help," she said quietly.

"Shoot."

"You're going to call me a city slicker and tell me I'm an idiot," she said wryly, and noted with amusement that he didn't rush to deny that.

"If we're going to have a serious talk, you'd better shuck those sandals, roll up your pant legs and dip your feet in the creek."

"That's a prerequisite to a serious talk?"

"Backwoods custom," he confirmed.

They ate with platters of steak on their laps and pants rolled up Tom Sawyer style, bare feet perched on stones in the creek. Just before the sun went down, the breeze died and a somnolent heat invaded the shadows. The warmth wouldn't last long, Grant told her. Nights always chilled down in the Upper Peninsula.

She was so relaxed that she nearly jumped sky-high when a toad popped next to her in the water, making Grant chuckle. That was enough laziness anyway. She sprang to her feet, embarrassingly aware of how close she'd come to falling asleep after dinner. Either the wine and a full stomach added up to a drugged sensation of well-being or the man next to her was a terrible influence. Kathryn suspected the latter. Grant was leaning against an old whitewood, his legs crossed and a glass of wine propped on his raised knee. He hadn't removed his crooked grin for an hour.

"So you're going to tell me your city slicker idea?"

"Yes." Efficiently she gathered up their plates and silver to rinse them in the stream. "I want to free my minks."

"Pardon?"

"You heard me. The property...I don't strictly have to worry about the property this instant. I can fix up the cabin, put the place up for sale and wait. But I have to do something with the animals."

"I understand that."

"There's no one in town who raises them or wants to raise them—not for money, not even for free. The best offer I had was someone willing to take them off my hands by killing them." She felt like a pioneer woman, scraping sand on the plates to get them clean in the stream. "I'm not doing that."

"There are probably animal ranchers around just a little distance from here. You've only been here for two days," he reminded her.

"I know. And that's what I assumed I'd do when I came here—find someone who was already into raising animals for pelts, and then give him a few more. Only I've thought about that all day, and it's not what I want to do." Waving the dripping plates to dry them, she carried them back to his wicker basket. "I want to let them go—and you don't have to tell me that's easier said than done. I know. Obviously they've been raised in captivity. I can't just open the cage doors and say shoo. They'd die if they were left in the wild. But couldn't they be sort of...decivilized, taught to cope in their natural environment, taught to follow up their natural instincts again?''

"Kate—"

"Everywhere I turned in town, I was told you were the one who knew about animals. There was no one else I could ask but you.'' Grant had already treated Baby to her own steak, but Kathryn knelt down to offer her two additional bones. After that she glanced up. Their little fire was dying down. The sun was gone, and ebon shadows deepened in the woods. Before it turned pitch-black, she picked up a few sticks to add to the fire and then wandered around looking for more.

Grant opened his mouth to say something but forgot what it was. She was still barefoot, and she'd lost the rubber band holding her French braid together. Golden strands of silk wisped around her cheeks and throat. Her makeup had worn off. Now her lips were a natural coral, her face softer than cream. One of her pant legs was still rolled up at the knee, the other had slipped down to midcalf. He loved the look of her.

He'd heard what she'd said about decivilizing the minks. All he could think about was decivilizing Kathryn. Sleek and sophisticated, she was beautiful. Natural, like this, sensual and easy and unselfconscious, like this, she was breathtaking.

"I didn't think you were such a do-gooder," he said.

"Pardon?''

"Look, Kate. You live in Chicago, safe and sound, quite a distance from the realities of survival living. It's easy to get all righteous at the idea of killing an animal to get a coat. But you eat red meat, honey. An animal has to be killed so you can have that meat on your table. That's just life. Reality. Survival."

Kneeling down in front of him, she shook her head. "Come on, those aren't the same things at all. People have to eat to live, but they don't have to kill an animal to stay warm, at least not in this day and age. These days there are hundreds of man-made fabrics that easily protect people from the elements."

"That kind of argument won't wash. Any time you start talking about 'man-made,' you talk about far more dangerous wildlife killers than anything as innocuous as mink ranching. Look at plastics and how they've killed marine life. Look at the incredible list of animals on the endangered species because of man. Any time you add something artificial to the ecological system, you talk about a death trap for the animals affected by that environment. Sentimentality about your minks is out of place. A mink coat is warm, sturdy, lasting. A coat that's well made and well cared for should last a person a lifetime. My best guess is that far fewer animals are killed to keep a woman warm by mink than to keep her warm by wearing a lifetime of man-made products."

Kathryn placed her hands on her knees and glared at him. Sometime soon she was going to mention that a mere lazy backwoodsman shouldn't be so familiar with talk about ecological systems. For now, she settled for a level, "Fine. You wear mink coats yourself, do you?"

He gave a slash of wicked grin. "Nope."

"Then why are you arguing with mé?"

His tone was frank, but not unkind. "To make sure you understand that idealism is out of place as far as 'saving' your mink. And your uncle built up equity in the animals and equipment. You're talking about throwing that away."

"Yes," she agreed.

He raised an eyebrow. "I would think the chance to sock away a little security would be important to you."

"It is." And desperately always had been.

"There'll be some mink ranchers around who'll take on the animals and equipment. Just not as fast as you want to move. You want to go back to your Chicago store, you go back to your Chicago store. I'll handle it for you."

"No." She sighed. "I just don't want any part of it, Grant. I want to set them free."

"Why?"

"Not because of principles," she said uncomfortably. She felt pinned under his dark, steady eyes. He was no longer smiling. "I agree that I don't know enough about all the conservationist and preservationist and 'save the minks' or 'not save the minks' issues to make any kind of judgment."

"So?"

"So I don't care about principles." She let out a huge breath. "Look, if I needed these animals to survive, maybe I could manage to feel differently, but I don't need a coat and I don't need an income that comes in this way. My uncle was entitled to make his own choices. I'm just talking about mine. It's the cages, Grant. You put anything behind bars and it turns mean. People do it to themselves all the time, lock themselves up behind rules and emotional control and responsibilities. Maybe that's the way it has to be, but there's no *reason* to do it to these animals, no reason they can't be free. Can you try to understand? Lately I've felt like rattling my own cage bars too darn often. I just can't do it to them!"

Grant's dark eyes glinted warm and bright. "I hate to tell you this, honey, but you seem to be reacting rather emotionally to the whole issue."

"I know that," she said irritably.

"I could have sworn you took a lot of pride in being a strongly rational woman."

"I *am*."

His voice turned husky and low. "Come over here, Kathryn Price."

Four

———

She had no intention of moving closer, but Grant didn't give her a chance. His hands encircled her waist, and he pulled her back and then down. She was suddenly facing the sky from flat on her back. Cavemen never won brownie points from Kathryn, never mind that her heart was suddenly beating like a semi engine on permanent rev. Stretched out, leaning on an elbow next to her, Grant appeared as relaxed as a sleepy panther, and she didn't care for the look in his eyes. She could probably have been the first woman president and not earned that gleam of pride and pleasure.

"A totally irrational emotional decision, to free those minks of yours," he murmured. "I didn't think you had it in you, Kate."

"Is that supposed to be a compliment?"

"I am overwhelmingly proud of you."

"I can't tell you how thrilled that makes me. Let me up, Kaufman."

He shook his head.

"Immediately." Her tone was still pleasant.

"I'm not going to jump you," he scolded. "I just think it's a good idea for you to relax. Practice, Kate. Five minutes without moving. If that's too much, go for four. I swear it won't kill you."

For a few moments she was silent. In the distance their fire spit and crackled. A restless wind swept the tops of the trees. She could feel the heat of Grant's palm on her stomach, the brace of his thigh against hers. She saw the lazy mischief in his eyes. She also saw something else.

Defusing dynamite could be a touchy business. Very odd things seemed to set this man off. Perhaps most men could be forgiven for responding to a flash of skin, a certain smile. Grant seemed to take fire from women who made sudden, foolish, impulsive decisions.

Worse than that, his closeness affirmed the pleasure of impulsiveness. Shock victims had steadier pulses. "Don't," she had the sense to say.

"Don't what?"

"We tried cuddling this morning," she reminded him. "Neither of us gained much out of that but a lot of irritation. You don't want an affair with me any more than I want one with you."

"True," he agreed. "But do you assume every man's going to make a pass who wants you to sit next to him?"

"Yes."

"That's a lot of ego on your part, Kate," he chided her.

"That line might work on a seventeen-year-old. Now…either we're talking minks or I'm going home. It's a simple enough question—are you willing to help me with the animals, or aren't you?"

He was thinking about it, thinking about what it would take to put the wild back in the minks. Thinking about what it would take to put a little wild in the minx.

The pulse in her throat throbbed. He liked that. A woman without nerves was boring, insensitive. Kathryn could never be either. She was tense, prepared to mutiny if he came an inch closer. Like a wild mink, her lithe, slight body was luxuriously soft. Like a wild mink, she was all spit and sass and fight. She'd had to be. Damn, he understood.

It worried him that she didn't know how to play. It touched him that she'd admitted to being irrational on the subject of her animals. And it disturbed him that he couldn't seem to keep his hands off a woman who represented everything he'd locked out of his life.

"Grant…" The warning in her voice was as clear as the last call in the ring before the wrestling match.

"Darn it, I'm thinking about your minks, Kate," he said irritably. "Can't you trust a man for two seconds?"

"Many men, yes. In fact, most."

That wounded. "I said I wouldn't jump you."

"Yes. Politicians sell promises, too."

He'd never met a more difficult woman. Deliberately he began a long, boring dissertation on the practical difficulties of freeing her minks. For openers, "decivilizing" the animals wouldn't just take time, but expense and hassle. They'd have to build outside pens in the minks' natural environment. They'd have to trap live prey to teach the animals to hunt. Since minks were night creatures, the two of them would have to work night hours to guard them, because all kinds of natural predators would be drawn to the outside cages and live prey. Finally, Kate would have to stay more than her sacred two weeks. He had no idea how long the project would take, but he guessed between a month or two.

Beyond the practical problems was the more basic issue of real survival for the critters. For Kate to idealize the concept of freeing them would be a mistake. They were safe in a cage; there were no guarantees any of them would survive in the wild. She'd have to accept that.

Kathryn listened, watching him. As the feeling of danger disappeared, her heartbeat changed from a racing beat to a slow, languid rhythm. The more objections Grant voiced, the more she could see he was becoming fascinated with the subject. She'd already guessed that he felt passionately about freedom. His brows were forming a shelf over his eyes from concentration. He had a habit of running a hand through the right side of his hair, not the left. The right side always looked more rumpled.

She wondered what he would look like combed and tamed, in pinstripes and wing tips. She kept worrying about why she was lying next to him and not moving.

For no reason she looked up, seeing a ceiling of leaves. Close to the forest floor, fireflies played a lazy game of tag, a spark of light here, then there. The creek gurgled close by, once silver in sunlight, now a rippling black satin ribbon by night. Their fire was no more than a bed of orange coals.

She closed her eyes and smelled the earth, pines, sweet woodsmoke. On this crisp, cool night, Grant was close, warm and solid. His tenor was little more than a whisper, and gradually a wine-warm, lethargic feeling spread through her limbs. It took her a long time to identify the feeling: she felt safe.

She couldn't remember feeling safe, not as a child, seldom as an adult. There had always been wolves at the door, battles to fight, mountains to climb. She couldn't have even climbed a porch step at the moment. Danger was feeling stress seep out of her body and the feel of a callused palm smoothing a strand of hair from her cheek while she did nothing to stop it.

"You're so tired you can't hold your head up," he murmured. "Dammit, Kate, when's the last time you had eight hours of sleep?"

Her eyes blinked open. "I was listening," she insisted sleepily. And she had been, with part of her mind. He'd been talking about the different nature of creatures. A rabbit, once caged, could never survive in the wild again. He believed her minks might make it, simply because their nature had always been essentially wild, untamable. The difference seemed to be in an animal's will, its need to be free.

All she could think of was that Grant could understand the need to be free if anyone could. "You've decided to help me," she said quietly.

"Don't be silly. I was always going to help you. Kate?"

"Hmm?"

"I'm afraid I'm going to have to kiss you."

So was she...afraid, but not surprised. She shivered when she felt the prickly graze of his beard, and then his smooth, warm mouth found hers. She closed her eyes. Her hands laced through his thick dark hair, enjoying the vibrant, bristly texture. It was insane, of course, to let this happen. It was insane to feel safe in this man's arms.

But she did. She felt soft and safe and small, surrounded by cold, except where Grant was. Surrounded by darkness, except where Grant was. The wolves were still there, the battles still waiting...she was so tired of them. Just once, just for a minute, she let the luxury of a fantasy become real. Grant was strong and hard and his mouth unbearably sensual. There had never been another man who'd stirred her like this one. He was an alluringly sexual man. For a moment she was no more, and no less, than a woman.

"We won't take this too far," he whispered.

"No."

"Just a kiss."

"Yes." But it was like flying on the tail of a comet, caught up in heat and light and speed. His lips found her bare throat. Her throat burned. His palms swept down her spine to her hips. Everywhere he touched turned hot. Her limbs tangled around him when his callused hand stroked her abdomen, her ribs. Then it claimed her breast with impossible gentleness. Drowning was delicious. She'd never guessed.

He could take her, he knew, and he wanted nothing more. His breath was harsh from wanting. He needed her under him, bare. He wanted her long legs wrapped around him and her hands in his hair, and he wanted to hear her cry out in an explosion of passion. He'd hoped to loosen her emotions, but he'd never expected it. He'd hoped for a small taste of the private, secret Kate. He'd never expected the powerful hunger she'd touched off in him.

She was so wild, so sweet.

She was so exhausted.

He tore his lips away from hers and wrapped his arms around her, holding her still and close, her face buried in his shoulder and his arousal pressed torturously against her. Sometime in the far future he was going to find this humorous. There was a word for the condition he was in. As a teenage boy, he'd suffered a lot from that condition, but never as a grown man. A grown man knew better than to invite desire that wasn't going to be satisfied, and to stay pressed against her went past torture and moved right into insanity.

"Grant?"

"Sssh." The sound came out angry. He took a long breath, but he didn't move. "Nothing's going to happen, Kate. Nothing. Just let me hold you."

She sighed against him. "I don't understand."

"Sssh." His lips brushed her forehead. "Close your eyes."

They couldn't stay in the woods. By midnight the temperature had dropped ten degrees, and dew was starting to dampen the ground. He had to move them, but he looked at Kathryn one last time before stirring.

Her face was stark white in the darkness, her lashes like ink against her cheeks. One of her arms was draped across his neck, limp and heavy. Her right leg was tucked between his, bent at the knee.

He doubted she'd stir even if a bomb dropped. For the past hour he'd had the uncontrollable urge to shake her for ever allowing herself to get into this state of exhaustion. For the same past hour he'd tried to figure out why he hadn't made love to her when he had had the chance . . . but he knew why.

A woman drugged with wine, darkness and exhaustion couldn't make clear choices. When he made love to Kate, he wanted her awake, aware and damned sure it was what she wished to do.

Where all that honor came from, Grant had no idea. It irritated him. Carefully he shifted, draping her with the cotton blanket before he lifted her. Baby groaned when he clicked his teeth for her to follow them. He left the basket and Kathryn's shoes. They'd wait until morning.

The cabin was a good quarter mile from the creek. Kate was light, but not that light. It would have been a lot easier to carry her fireman style, but then she would undoubtedly have wakened. Grant was prepared to murder anyone or anything that woke her up for the next ten hours.

It wasn't as if he didn't know he was in trouble. When a man felt swamped by instincts of protection and possession, he should have the sense to run for cover. Kate was more than capable of protecting herself, and he knew that she wouldn't appreciate possessiveness in a man or anyone else. He also knew better than to get involved with a duchess.

Unfortunately there was more to Kathryn than the duchess. He'd tasted the minx in Kate. He wanted more.

Kathryn woke to the smell of blueberries and the feel of a warm, wet tongue in her ear. She swatted the tongue, her eyes squinting open against a dazzling sun . . . and the face of a bloodhound inches from her own.

"Now, I'd scold her, but I was just about to wake you up anyway. Sleep's fine, but it's about time you had some food."

She pushed back her hair, hoping vaguely that she was suffering from some new form of shock. The last thing she remembered was draping herself all over Grant like paint to plaster. That memory was debilitating enough, but the cold, dark woods had miraculously metamorphosed into her uncle's cabin loft. The high-noon sun was slanting through the window, and a seventy-pound bloodhound was trying to sneak onto her bed.

If that wasn't enough to startle a woman, finding a man standing at the stairs carrying a tray of blueberry pancakes would have done it. Grant was wearing a beard, jeans and a lot of dark chest hair, but nothing else. Worse than that, her own jeans seemed to be bunched in a ball on the dresser, which seemed to imply she wasn't wearing them.

She wasn't.

"Now, don't get all nervous. You couldn't very well sleep in tight jeans all night."

Grant leaned over her, fussed over straightening the faded quilt on her lap and set down the tray with a scowl. She noted a stack of steaming blueberry pancakes ample enough to feed a lumberjack, the folded napkin, and the ice cubes floating in what certainly smelled like freshly squeezed orange juice. More than that, she noticed Grant. Every muscle in his body was tense, as if he was ready to defend himself against an entire army.

"I didn't touch a hair on your body, and yes, I slept here. Downstairs. On the couch." His tone reeked belligerence. "By the time we got back here, it was well past midnight, and I knew the minks had to be fed in the morning. If you want to make something else of that, go ahead."

She said nothing. Still studying him, she slid a
forkful of pancakes into her mouth. The crepe-thin
pancakes were tantalizingly delectable. Grant was even
more so. Just above his beard, a slash of red colored
his cheeks. His eyes never met hers.

"You've slept fourteen hours," he said gruffly.
"Talk about comatose. I checked on you three times
to make sure you were still breathing. Do you realize
what time it is? *Noon*. And drink your orange juice!"

Obediently she reached for her orange juice.

"And say something, for heaven's sake. I figured
you'd wake up all huffy, ready to make a big mountain out of a molehill because I stayed here."

"Thank you, Grant," she said softly. Laughter
danced in her eyes. His arm was raised in midair in the
middle of some violently defensive gesture; it dropped
like a limp leaf.

"What?"

Pushing aside the tray and dragging the blanket with
her, she knee-walked to the end of the bed, raised
herself and kissed his cheek. "Thank you," she repeated gently. "For taking care of me. For the pancakes. For all of it."

Every tense muscle in his body turned to silly putty.
He saw blue eyes, sunlight-yellow tangled hair. The
kiss was no more than she'd have given a puppy. He
felt like a man entering into a battle completely un-
armed. Darn woman. Every time he thought he had
her figured out, she confused him again. He'd been
positive she'd be upset at the idea of his taking care of
her.

Still holding the quilt to her waist, Kathryn reached into the bureau next to the bed for fresh clothes. She made a tent of the quilt, using her head for the pole, to both undress and redress. A shower would have to wait. "I understand why you're feeling a little touchy—because of last night," she called out conversationally. "We do seem to have this small problem every time we're together. Have you noticed?"

There was a moment's silence, and then his low, "Maybe I didn't hear you right."

"Sure you did." Still under the quilt, she tugged the cotton sweater over her head, then bit her lower lip. Even the look of Grant contained the tingle of something new, special, secret. What she'd felt with him the night before made her wonder if she'd ever been in love before. She didn't know who or what he was... only that last night he'd proven himself capable of tenderness and trust and caring. No one in her life had ever offered her those things for free.

She was afraid that it mattered too much, which was why she now carefully kept her voice light and breezy. "You're not even sure you like me, Grant. And frankly, that beard of yours scratches like a bramble bush. I don't want to be involved with you, any more than you want to be involved with me." Pulling on jeans was an awkward process, particularly when she was trying to listen for a response. There was none. "Look. If you want to get out of helping me with the minks, you can."

"No."

"Really, I would understand—"

"Kate, would you get out from under that darned quilt so I can hear you?"

Fully dressed, her sweater tucked neatly at her waist, she pushed off the quilt and glanced at him. He was too darn big for the tiny loft. His gaze lanced her face, and she felt the vibrations of raw male virility, primitive power, powder-keg emotions.

He badly needed taming, she thought fleetingly. A small thank-you and a little feminine honesty seemed to upset the man all out of proportion. Perhaps, deep inside her, she was equally upset. Damnation. Grant was an unemployed, seemingly irresponsible man with a long, lazy streak. She couldn't possibly care about him . . . except she did.

The previous night this arrogant caveman had made her do something that she couldn't—and didn't want to—take back. However foolish, however impulsive, her lazy vagrant had touched a spring of life in her, a yearning, a need. Yes, he was the wrong man . . . but what if there was no one else, ever? What if she just kept growing hard and tough and cold and there was no one to unlock the cage doors on Kathryn the woman?

"You're sure you want to help me?" she repeated.

"I told you I would and I will. Kate—"

"We'd better get going then, don't you think?" she interrupted smoothly. "You said something about building outside pens. I'll have to buy the fencing, and you'll have to tell me how much we need and where I can buy it. And after that . . ."

She deliberately rambled on, undoubtedly coming across as a drill sergeant, but she couldn't seem to stop. Moving around him, she made the bed, then straightened the room and whisked a brush through her hair at the same time, knowing the frenetic activity annoyed him, but unable to stop that, too.

By the time she gathered up the tray and was ready to go downstairs, Grant was still blocking the narrow loft stairway. He took the tray from her hands. There was just a moment when she felt a shiver of sexual awareness because of his closeness, when she glimpsed frustration in his eyes and determination in his set mouth.

In that speck of time, she knew exactly how crazy it was to even consider being involved with him. She also remembered how his arms had felt around her the night before. Grant would have her believe he was a self-sufficient loner. But if he'd freed something dangerous and vulnerable in her last night, he'd also kissed like a man who craved loving and touching.

"Ready?" she asked lightly. "We've got a lot to do."

"More than you know," he answered flatly.

"You *are* going to get around to wearing clothes today, aren't you?"

He shot her a look filled with patience. So that's how it's going to be, she thought fleetingly, and grinned. The poor man was used to having things his own way. He had a few shocks coming. She had no intention of jumping off a mountain alone.

* * *

"All right. What's next?" Kathryn set down her hammer after pounding the last stake in the ground. After three long days, the fencing was finally finished.

She straightened and stretched. Chicago had never seemed so far away. Muscles that she didn't know she had groaned. Grit had collected under her few remaining long fingernails, and the sun beat down on her arms and neck. For years she'd spent her days worrying about bills and fashion styles and competition. Now all she could seem to fret over were her minks.

While she kneaded the small of her back with her hands, she surveyed the land around the creek. Individual wire-fence pens were strewn from here to kingdom come. Her checkbook would have suffered less if they could have put the animals in one large cage, but Grant had told her it wasn't possible. Minks were distinctly territorial, and they would have simply killed one another.

Minks were also natural thieves. Too lazy to build their own homes, they preferred to steal an empty fox den or muskrat house. Two weeks ago she could have cared less about such a detail. Now it was critical to know if her animals were to survive. While she'd pounded in stakes and unwrapped wire fencing, Grant had taken on the dirtier job of creating shelters and water holes. Wearing gloves to reduce his human scent, he'd lugged hollow logs, shoveled out nests and stocked the makeshift homes with leaves and twig "bedding."

It was done now. Each fenced-in pen had a shelter and a water hole. The plan was to slowly acclimatize the minks to living outside. At first they'd be fed the diet they were accustomed to, then gradually the proportion of raw foods they would naturally find in the wild would be increased. Grant told her he'd set traps to catch their natural prey alive—frogs, fish, field mice, birds, rabbits. The idea of locking the small creatures in with the minks to teach them to hunt sounded gruesome to Kathryn.

But one thing at a time. She pushed a stray lock of hair from her forehead and glanced at Grant. "Can we start transporting the minks?"

"We'll do that tomorrow." Grant reached for his shirt where he'd left it under a tree.

"Can't we do it now? It wouldn't take that long to carry the cages out here."

It was four in the afternoon. It would take hours to carry out the cages, and the miniature slave driver in front of him had a sunburned nose. Buttoning his shirt, Grant glanced at her, and couldn't help grinning. Her silk shirt was rolled up to her forearms and tied at the ribs. Her jeans had a rip in one knee and a designer streak of dirt on one thigh.

He was extraordinarily proud of her. She wasn't afraid to get her hands dirty and didn't have an ounce of vanity. Putting a little wild back in Kathryn wasn't nearly as hard as he'd thought . . . as long as they were talking about that one arena—work. "We'll bring the animals out tomorrow," he repeated.

"Why?"

"Because it's time for iced tea, Kate," he said patiently.

She nodded. "You're thirsty. You go ahead and get a drink. I'll—"

"No."

She nodded again. "Well, after we've both had a little break, we can—"

"No." It was like dealing with a toddler. Lengthy, rational explanations were wasted. Simple noes were more effective. Kathryn simply didn't understand that every single day didn't have to involve fifteen hours of work. "I've got sun tea sitting on my porch. My place is less than a quarter-mile walk from here."

"Your place?" She swiftly shook her head. "That's not necessary. If we're done for the day, I'll just go home."

"And sneak back out to work like you did the past two days? No dice." He grabbed the shovel and ax to carry home, well aware that Kathryn had avoided any chance of being alone with him in circumstances that didn't involve sun, sweat and exhausting labor. "I figure it's about time you saw my place," he said lazily. "Give you a good chance to put your duchess on."

Warily she put her hands on her hips. "What duchess?"

"You. You're the duchess. Especially when you ask me one of those tactfully worded questions about when and if I've ever had a serious job." He grinned. "It just kills you, doesn't it, Kate? That I don't work for a living?"

"I never meant to pry," she said stiffly. Increasingly she couldn't believe that Grant had no ambition, no goals beyond living for the moment.

"Sure you did. And by now I figure you've got my place pictured as having no clocks and no curtains, with mold growing up the walls—a real lazy man's hideaway. Afraid to find out for sure?"

"Afraid? Of course not. The only reason I haven't taken you up on your invitation to see your place—"

"I can hardly wait to hear this," he told the sky.

"—is because I didn't want to taint anything. Being female and all. I mean...I did pretty much figure your place as a big-deal male dominion, and you never know, Grant. I might touch something sacredly male by mistake...."

He gave her a long-suffering look. She gave him one back. Working with him, as she could have guessed before they'd started, was impossible. He moved slow to her manic. He believed in two-hour lunches and used any excuse to take a break. Other men brought her roses. Grant brought her gifts of some foul-smelling mosquito repellant and a ridiculous straw hat that he actually expected her to wear.

He also, as he did now, took touch for granted. His arm dragged across her shoulder as they reached the open meadow past his creek. Tall grasses swayed in the fretful breeze, blending with splashes of yellow and blue wildflowers. "I'm going to kill you before this is over, Kate," he said gravely.

"Assuming you're still standing."

"You drive me nuts. On a minute-by-minute basis."

"Yes." She felt constantly thrown off-balance. They argued incessantly. The more they argued, the more she had the terrible feeling they were beginning to like each other. That didn't make sense. Neither did hugs between adversaries, but the weight of his arm on her shoulder felt disturbingly natural.

"Did you notice the anemones?"

"Yes." Yet another thing that annoyed her. He claimed she was unperceptive and made a big business out of stopping work to teach her about wildflowers, birds, wildlife. No one had ever accused her of a lack of perception before and the label hurt her feelings. It also wasn't true. All five of her senses were disastrously open and aware every time she was around him.

He removed his arm from her shoulder when they reached a narrow, tree-crowded section of the path. She felt bereft...and silly. It wasn't easy to explain to her conscience why she craved the touch of a man without a future, without ambition, without an ounce of drive in his soul. Still, the sexual vibrations kept sneaking up on her like a summer storm. She tried to banish them with a little humor. Maybe her psyche had always had a few buried fantasies about macho, elemental types. Maybe she'd been without sex too long. Maybe she was nuts.

At thirty-one chemistry was hardly new in her life. Sex was a need, a simple thing. She'd always believed that, like everything else, it took work to make it good, not romance, not candlelight, but a serious effort at sensitivity and learning one's partner's needs and vulnerabilities.

Grant shot all that to hell and made her feel tricked. She hadn't known that desire was a terrifyingly potent power all by itself. Or guessed how obsessive her own curiosity could be about a man who claimed to abhor work and had labored harder than any three men over the past few days. About a man who claimed a distaste for responsibility and had taken on her project without thanks or payment or hesitation. About a man who believed he needed no one, even though she'd felt a depth of loneliness in him that matched her own.

She stopped dead when they came into the clearing on the other side of the woods.

Grant took one look at her face and said wryly, "Maybe it's lucky you weren't expecting the Taj Mahal?"

Five

When she pushed open the door, Kathryn felt as if she were stepping back in time. His cabin wasn't large. A fieldstone wall divided the two main rooms, with a fireplace that opened onto both. On one side there was a baking pit and a raised hearth cluttered with wrought-iron pots. She saw no television, no radio, none of the accumulation of things that would have brought the place into the twentieth century.

She couldn't stop touching—the hand-hewn oak table, Grant's leather jacket hanging from a hook, the whetstone on a wheel in the corner. Expecting male clutter, she saw austerity and neatness. Expecting creature comforts, she saw deer rifles, an ax, fishing poles, knives—the tools of a man who hunted his own food. She could smell linseed oil, wood and leather. A huge wooden bowl sat on a table, filled with sweet cherries; she could smell those, too.

The austerity was broken by color. An antique lantern had red glass, and a huge rug on one wall had an Indian pattern of rich red, gold and blue. His bed was curtained off with a wool blanket, also red. Most of his clothes were hanging, and she saw leathers, cottons and wools, all fabrics that might have existed a hundred years before, not a hint of polyester or blends.

"The bottom drawer has underwear. I mean, if you're determined to be nosy, Kate, you might as well go whole hog."

"Oh, hush, Kaufman." She knew he was behind her. He'd brought in a pitcher of sun tea from the porch; she heard the clink of glasses. "You built it all, didn't you? The house. Even the furniture."

He nodded. "Stone by stone and log by log."

"I don't understand you."

The comment appeared to both startle and amuse him. One of his brows cocked in an inverted V. "What's to understand or not understand?"

She motioned everywhere in general and mused absently, "My apartment is in peach. When I look out at night, I can see Chicago's night lights. My carpet is cream and my living room has a lot of glass, a lot of chrome." She shook her head. Her voice was light, but her tone was serious. "I love it. It's exactly what I want, exactly what I've worked hard for—the luxuries. You really don't give a hoot about any of that, do you?''

Again she appeared to have surprised Grant. He handed her a glass of iced tea and led her past the main room. Afternoon sunlight poured through the west windows onto oak bookshelves and oversize furniture—two of her could have fit in any chair. ''In principle, I'm living without the civilized trappings,'' he said dryly. ''In reality, there's a back room with two propane-run freezers, stocked with venison, rabbit and duck. And I'm too sissy to make it without hot water. There's a generator-run water pump and a tub in the bathroom big enough for a luxury-loving sheikh.''

''Still. You're really set up to be completely self-sufficient, aren't you?'' She folded herself in the corner of his long brown couch, tucking her legs under her.

''Give or take a little bartering. I barter for my propane by cutting wood. And clothes. Jeans wear out, so I trade a side of venison maybe, or do a little carpentry.'' Grant settled in a huge wooden rocker, draping a leg over one side.

She took a sip of tea and regarded him over the rim of the glass. Her features were relaxed, but her heart kicked up a disturbing beat. She shouldn't have come here.

She'd hoped that seeing his place would put paid to the sexual draw she felt for him. The opposite was true. Contrary to everything he'd led her to believe, he hadn't chosen the easy, lazy way, but possibly the hardest of life-styles. He provided for himself; he depended on no one. There was no question that he was a renegade, but Grant was also a free man, self-reliant, independent.

All her life she'd valued those things. No amount of cream carpeting or nest eggs or air-conditioning ever added up to real security. She'd been successful, but she was still terrified of the wolf at the door.

"Great balls of fire," Grant murmured lazily. "The woman has been quiet for all of five minutes. Is the roof going to cave in?"

"It might."

"You make me nervous when you think too long, Kate."

With his head tilted back and one foot absently keeping the rocker in slow motion, Grant couldn't look less nervous. Or afraid, she thought fleetingly. He really wasn't afraid of anything. He was a man who would provide and protect, and to hell with anyone else's rules.

The only thing that didn't gel—the itch that kept nagging at her—was an awareness that it took a strong man to say to hell with the rules. Weak men didn't have the courage. Lazy men didn't have the energy.

She hesitated, studying him. "You don't miss any of it?"

"Miss what?"

Her eyes never left his face. "Schedules. The rat race. Power, ambition." She said slowly, "You had a lot of power, didn't you, Grant? And a lot of people under your control. I don't have any idea why you dropped out, but you're never going to convince me you started out as a hermit backwoodsman.''

Grant set down his glass, lurched to his feet and slowly started walking toward her. She watched with almost detached interest as he leaned forward and boxed her in with strong arms on both sides of her. "You're an unbelievably perceptive woman, Kate."

"Did I strike a nerve? Gosh, I'm sorry."

She wasn't sorry. Her smile was purely feminine. As if he were watching himself jump for a trapeze bar without a net, he reached closer to touch her mouth. Kissing Kate was always trouble. Like now. She tasted like mint and lemon tea, and her tongue was as cool as ice. Her throat arched like a kitten for cream, and every nerve in his body came alive.

The damn woman had avoided his touch for three days; now she showed responsiveness when he wanted to talk to her. He lifted his mouth. "You did not strike a nerve... but by bringing you here, I was hoping to strike one of yours."

"How so?"

He straightened, dark eyes level on hers. "When I was twenty-four, I started a small manufacturing company that shouldn't have had a chance in hell of making it. I was too young, and I was short on capital, labor, and heaven knows, experience. The business was making solvents for machine parts—nothing you've ever heard of or could possibly have any interest in. That doesn't matter. I think it only made it because I loved the damn thing into succeeding. Like thinking a puppy won't grow, the one business got bigger and gradually turned into three separate companies. By the time I was thirty, I had one healed ulcer, more money than I knew what to do with and a doctor's prognosis that I was headed for an early heart attack. I loved it, Kate. I had drive just like you have drive, ambition just like you have ambition. Are you hearing me?''

"Yes," she said softly.

"Don't do it, Kathryn Price. You can be on that roller coaster so long that you forget what it's like on the ground. Killing yourself for a dollar isn't worth it.''

Her tone was instantly defensive. "It was never exactly for the money—''

"No. It's for the kick when you climb one step higher. It's for the security that's supposed to come with things, and never does. It's for the challenge. Do you think I don't understand? But you suddenly come to a point where your entire life is business, where you eat, sleep and drink problems. Where you talk yourself into believing you're still having fun but somehow you can't remember the last time you laughed.''

His gentle tenor upset her more than she wanted to admit. He understood too much—and not enough. Her heart had been scolding her for months to get off the treadmill. But how could she without risking everything she'd worked for and the security she desperately valued?

Grant was leaning against the windowsill now. Sunlight put dust in his beard and streaks of silver in his hair. He had such beautiful eyes, and she felt the same turbulent stirrings she always had when she was near him. He grated against values she thought were secure, intruded on private grounds where she wanted no one. But he also made her feel a confusing mess of emotions. Want, empathy. Fear, caring, vulnerability.

She set down her iced tea glass with a clunk. If he really thought he could upset her world while sitting in his own glass house, he was mistaken. She motioned around her. "So this is your answer?" she asked quietly. "You dropped out, Grant. You've made it your own way, but I don't believe it's that simple. Maybe you don't miss the tension, the clocks, the pressure. But what do you do with the drive, the need for challenge? Are you asking me to believe you're totally content with your choices?"

She saw something flicker in his eyes. "There's nothing in heaven or hell that could make me go back to the way I used to live," he said shortly. "This place is exactly what I am, who I am now. Have no illusions."

"Which doesn't answer the question. Are you happy?"

"More than you, Kathryn Price." His tone turned smooth and easy, like water rippling over stones. "I didn't bring you here to talk about me. I brought you here to shake you up, disturb you. I want to disturb you. I've wanted to disturb you from the moment I met you." He murmured, "You have a dangerous habit of kissing like a woman saying yes, Kate. I think you want to be shaken up a bit. I think you need it.

Say **YES** to free gifts worth over $20.00

Say YES to a rendezvous with romance, and you'll get 4 classic love stories—FREE! You'll get an LCD digital quartz watch—FREE! You'll get a stylish ballpoint pen—FREE! And you'll get a delightful surprise—FREE! These gifts carry a value of over $20.00—but you can have them without spending even a penny!

MONEY-SAVING HOME DELIVERY

Say YES to Silhouette and you'll enjoy the convenience of previewing 6 brand-new books delivered right to your home every month. Each book is yours for only $2.24 — 26¢ less than the retail price, and there is no extra charge for postage and handling.

SPECIAL EXTRAS—FREE!

You'll get our monthly newsletter, packed with news of your favorite authors and upcoming books—FREE! You'll also get additional free gifts from time to time as a token of our appreciation for being a home subscriber.

Say YES to a Silhouette love affair. Complete, detach and mail your Free Offer Card today!

And the real reason I brought you here was to tell you I want you like hell—and that I'm coming after you. Not nice and slow and sweet like the past three days, but with everything I have.''

Such soft-spoken words shouldn't have had such power, yet warm honey suddenly flowed through her veins, and she couldn't look away from his dark, piercing gaze. The sky could have rained pins and neither would have noticed.

Heat flushed her cheeks. She gave him full credit for honor. He'd told her what he wanted and all the rules he intended to play by ahead of time. That was nice. She was tempted to pull out the hairs in his beard one by one.

She was also tempted to cross the room and wrap her arms around him. Foolish man. No relationship existed without commitment, responsibility, compromise. Did he think he was immune, that he was any less lonely than she was, less vulnerable because he'd carved out an isolated life for himself in the north woods?

He waited. She understood—he was fully expecting her to tell him to go to hell, and those words were on the tip of her tongue. He was offering nothing more than a short-term irresponsible affair, with no possibility of compromising his life-style to accommodate any kind of future between them.

He was offering her a taste of freedom, the tease of emotions, a moment in time in which only two people mattered— Maybe an incomparable excitement for now... followed by the crash of a loss when it was all over. No sane woman could possibly justify that choice.

"Kathryn—"

She stood up. "You are aware that someone's been wearing out their knuckles on your back door for the past five minutes?"

He didn't move. "I heard," he said impatiently. "I could care less. Whoever's there can wait—or preferably disappear."

"They won't have to do either. I'm answering your door. That's common courtesy, Kaufman, and when I get back I'll spell the words for you and give you a dictionary definition."

She took three long breaths on the way to the door, as if her lungs suddenly felt starved for air. Her common sense knew better than to tease danger. Grant fascinated, tempted, worried and lured her toward taking risks she knew were poor ones. She already knew that fire burned. She already guessed that intimacy with him would be special, maybe even unforgettable. So? She had a store in Chicago that wouldn't disappear. He didn't care. He didn't want anyone in his life who meant giving and giving up, responsibilities and ties.

No, she decided. That decision was precise, sure, and irrevocable...until she opened the back door. The little boy standing there was perhaps seven. He had a thatch of matted blond hair, overalls with patched knees and freckles blotched red from a crying streak. In his arms was a robin lying on its side, nestled carefully in a grass bed on a burlap sack.

He could hardly talk for the tears clogging his throat. "I need to talk to Mr. Kaufman, please."

Kathryn led him in, and for the next few minutes she watched from the doorway as Grant crouched on his haunches by the urchin's burlap bundle. Her cold-blooded predator—the one who'd sworn off responsibility and commitments, who boldly took what he wanted and the devil with everyone else—said gently, "Timmy, she's got a broken wing."

"Her mother pushed her out of the nest too soon! Can't you fix her? She's not so sick. I fed her a worm, and she ate it. See?"

Kathryn cringed when he reached a hand into his pocket and produced two grimy, wriggly earthworms.

"I got a whole bunch more," Timmy said. "See, I can feed her and take care of her and all. All you have to do is fix the wing, Mr. Kaufman. Can't you? Please?"

"We'll try." Grant looked into the little boy's eyes. "There's no guarantees, sport. What we'll do is our best—but only if we both agree ahead of time not to feel badly if she doesn't make it."

"I won't feel badly. At all. I'll feel great if she dies. See?" the little boy said, his grimy face momentarily wreathed in a smile that instantly died. "I got a cage to keep her safe until she can fly again. You remember when Rogan was run over? Because if you fixed Rogan, you must be able to fix a little old bird."

Kathryn had no idea who Rogan was, but it seemed the best of times to divert one blond-haired little boy with a bowl of cherries before he burst into tears again. Kneeling next to Timmy, she watched Grant whittle a tiny wood splint and tape it carefully to the bird's wing. Her would-be seducer had impossibly gentle hands. Her selfish, lazy renegade treated the small life with loving, precious care.

And he talked as he worked. "Now, give her water every hour or so from a medicine dropper. One drop at a time. And you can offer her those earthworms or a few bugs—but don't choke her with them. If she wants them, fine."

"I knew all that," Timmy announced.

"And you'll have to keep her in that cage of hers for at least a couple of weeks. For one thing, she shouldn't have the chance to fly, or she'll undo everything we're trying to accomplish. And for another, she can't protect herself right now, and a cage'll help keep other animals away from her."

"I'll keep all the animals away from her, even my sister," Timmy said gravely, and carefully scooped the bird back onto its burlap bed. "Now," he said firmly, "what do I owe you?"

Kathryn's lips parted in surprise, but Grant answered with ready seriousness. "If she makes it— which neither of us are counting on, because we both understand how badly she was hurt—then come this fall, maybe you can help me rake leaves for an hour. Fair?"

"Fair."

"And a hug for now," Grant said sternly.

Wielding the burlap bed in one arm, Timmy threw an arm around Grant's waist and squeezed tight. "We square now?"

"We're square now," Grant affirmed.

Timmy was gone in seconds. Kathryn looked at Grant and then moved swiftly to fetch both their empty iced tea glasses. Carrying them toward his kitchen area, she called over her shoulder, "Is the bird going to make it?"

"She'd damn well better, or I'll shoot her. He's counting on it," Grant said gruffly. He followed her as far as the wall next to his converted dry sink. "Never mind the bird, Kate—"

"You've got a gift for animals. I heard in town." She dried both glasses and then her hands on a towel. "Ever wanted to be a vet?"

"Are you still trying to find gainful employment for me?"

"No." She hung up his towel. "I think you've made it very clear how you feel about jobs, especially nine-to-five jobs. And other things." She whisked him a smile, her frostiest special. "I think we have a conversation to finish."

He stuffed his hands into his pockets. "Yes."

"If I understood everything you said—and I do want to be absolutely sure I've got this right—you want an affair. No strings, no ties, no hope for a future. Just sex, free and clear. Fun while we can, but no messy involvement, no emotional risks, no..." She waved her hand, "No love." She said the word as if it were naughty. "Neither of us have room in our lives for that kind of thing. We're both adults...so we both just walk away when the relationship isn't convenient anymore. Now...have I got it right?''

Grant raked a hand through his hair. "Wait a minute—"

"Oh, no. You said your terms. Now it's my turn to state mine." Her hand was on the doorknob when she turned with a smooth smile. "Shave off the beard, Kaufman. And tomorrow night—after our work day with the minks, of course—pick me up at eight."

She was gone faster than sunshine on a winter day.

All he could think of was that she'd done it to him again—twisted up everything he'd tried to say, made it seem...different, and left him confused and reeling like a man who'd just tackled a cyclone.

Standing by the open tailgate of Grant's pickup, Kathryn pulled on the heavy black gloves. This was their sixth transport of the morning, and thankfully the last. Billowing storm clouds were zooming in from the west. The temperature was as high as the humidity, and that had to be a million percent.

As soon as she fitted her fingers into the holes to lift the first cage, the mink leaped for her with a snarl. "Beauty is as beauty does, you little monster," she crooned. "I'm going to give you a mirror, Leroy. Maybe if you see how gorgeous you are, you won't be so mean."

"Kate, I told you I'd carry the rest."

"Might as well share the fun," she said blithely. Every cage had to be carted to its individual fenced-in pen, then each door opened. Kathryn had had visions that the minks would fly for freedom at the first opportunity, but most of them had done nothing so far except crouch in the back of their pens and snarl. And smell.

Leroy wasn't any different, though Kathryn stood by for a few extra seconds just in case. "What is it with you guys?" she murmured finally. "Skedaddle. Enjoy. Sunshine. Dirt. Free food. Your own hole. Why am I perspiring if this is no big thrill for you?"

Grant, behind her, carried two cages for her one. Kathryn had already noted that she seemed to be doing a lot of talking this morning, most of it nonsense, but then Grant didn't seem to be in much of a conversational mood. In fact, when the last cage was unloaded, he vaulted into the driver's seat of the truck and slammed the door. Low barometric pressure put a razor edge on some people's tempers, she considered judiciously. Or perhaps, given the heat and humidity, his beard itched. He certainly hadn't shaved it yet.

"So what's the next phase in this whole horrible plan?" she asked cheerfully.

"Setting traps to catch their natural prey."

Her stomach turned over. "All right. And what else besides that?"

"We start midnight shifts." Grant backed out of the rocky terrain and edged onto the highway. "Our pens are unfortunately going to attract every curious or hungry predator around. Our mink aren't really the problem—they're more trouble to a wolverine or a fox than they're worth, but those predators are going to like the idea of the free live food in the mink cages.''

"So what do we do about that?''

"*We* don't do anything. I will. Patrol, with a shotgun. It won't hurt the mink to learn fear of a gunshot sound, and from now on it's critical that they associate the smell of people with something frightening, evil, bad. In the meantime, though, an occasional blast will scare off potential predators. Hopefully.'' He glanced at her. "Kate, I warned you from the beginning that all of them might not make it.''

"I know you did.'' She tried to hold the eye-to-eye contact, but Grant instantly returned his attention to the road. So far that morning, his attention had been everywhere but on her. "It's darn complicated, isn't it?'' she asked cheerfully.

"What?''

"Freedom. Giving a thing freedom should be something nice, something easy. Instead, freeing a creature would seem to mean putting it at risk. A caged animal is the one who's safe.'' She caught another one of his wary glances. That one must have lasted a full second. "It's just the opposite with people, though, don't you think? I mean, I look at our life-styles, Grant. Yours is free, and mine is comparatively, well, caged. Sometimes I think I'm floating on risks—financial, social, legal, everything that has to do with a business. I envy you,'' she said.

"Kathryn—''

She heard the frog in his throat. That, too, seemed to have troubled him all morning. "You're free and clear, no risks, no involvements. I've thought a lot about what you said yesterday. I admit I can't imagine dropping everything and taking off for the north woods to skin deer—frankly, the thought makes me violently ill—but there's definitely something to be said for not needing other people, not making ties, reaching out for your own needs and not worrying about anyone else's."

"Kathryn, that wasn't what I was trying to—"

All morning she'd practiced interrupting him on the rare occasions he did try to talk. "Never mind. I never meant to get on that subject. We were talking about patrolling the woods at night. Naturally I'll help. I admit I can't shoot a gun—"

"Nor is there any need for you to learn—"

"But there was a guy in that bar. . . ." She frowned, then snapped her fingers. "Spenser! That was it. He offered to teach me."

Grant boosted the speed to seventy. "If anyone is going to teach you, I will."

"Well, fine," Kathryn said mildly. At the rate he was driving, it didn't take long to reach her front yard. Given their new midnight shift hours, the afternoon was free—although she did have orders to take a long nap. She had it in mind to mow the lawn instead.

Regardless of what she decided, Grant wouldn't be there to see her do it. Within minutes, the truck was speeding out of her driveway, leaving a trail of dust in its wake. She watched, hands on hips, until he was out of sight. He hadn't once, she was well aware, mentioned coming for her at eight o'clock that night. Being an old poker player herself, neither had Kathryn.

She hadn't taken an emotional risk in years. She was just beginning to understand that maybe Grant hadn't either. All morning long she'd tried her hardest to put him on edge. It seemed he wasn't so fond of talking about freedom when the subject related to her. Certainly, he'd become downright nervous when she chatted up wanting to take on some "free and clear" affairs. He'd tried to tell her that she'd completely misunderstood his little talk yesterday.

Kathryn hadn't misunderstood anything. Grant was too good, too strong a man to wallow in the solitude of the north woods for the rest of his life. Maybe the roller coaster of ambition wasn't the answer, but freedom without responsibility was a lonely road.

She'd made every effort to make him believe she was offering herself "free."

He hadn't liked it, and the dust still hadn't settled from his gunning of the engine as he'd driven out of the yard.

She was smiling when she walked into the cabin to make a late lunch... only her smile abruptly faltered. Her palms had been slick on the doorknob.

She cared. That was terrifying. Falling in love with the wrong man was even scarier. All her life she'd taken risks, terrible risks, serious risks... but not emotional ones.

Who was going to pick up the pieces if she was wrong about him?

Six

Stark naked, Grant leaned toward the bathroom mirror. Scissors, shaving cream and a straight razor lay on the counter next to him. He hadn't touched them.

It took a good long time for a man to grow a really decent beard.

Having a beard, of course, removed certain things from one's diet. Roasted marshmallows were a disaster. Meringue wasn't much better. Juicy peaches could be a serious problem. So could corn dripping with butter.

One time he'd been hunting in a snowstorm. His beard had frozen, and it had felt like walking around with a three-ton chin. And all that extra hair in hot weather was admittedly...well...hot. He was the first to admit the beard was a little out of hand right now, straggly, unkempt.

Jutting his chin forward for a better angle in the mirror, he picked up the scissors. He looked down with a feeling of unease when the first froth of black hair floated down into the sink. Ten minutes later he'd clipped enough so that he could apply shaving cream.

Twenty minutes later it was done. He squinted at his naked face, totally appalled. Baby scratched to get in the bathroom. He pulled open the door. The animal took one look at him and woofed. His own dog didn't even know him.

He scowled at his reflection as he toweled off the last of the shaving cream. He felt like the guy in the Bible who'd lost his strength when they cut off his hair.

He'd never expected Kathryn to say yes, and he didn't know how one small woman could mess everything up so fast. All he'd wanted to do was be honest with her, not give birth to a monster.

Honesty was knowing he couldn't keep his hands off Kate. Honesty was believing in his heart that he could give Kate that taste of freedom she needed. Honesty was wanting to woo Kate—not the duchess and not the businesswoman—but the lady capable of kissing with abandon, the lady capable of shucking her busy life for a hundred mangy minks. And honesty was not wanting to hurt her if she couldn't handle a short-term involvement, which was why he'd been so blunt—he'd wanted to give her every possible way out.

He frowned in the mirror. She'd blithely said yes like a virgin just unleashed from a chastity belt. He knew darn well she wasn't the kind to jump into a casual affair, and he'd never had only a fast trip to the nearest mattress in mind. Just because he didn't want a long-term entanglement didn't mean he was heartless. He cared enough to want to save her from the mistakes he had made. He cared enough to want to help her change because he believed that was what she wanted, too. She was the one who had jumped on the words "free and clear" as if they were gold. Darn it, maybe she needed a little freedom too much.

Fifteen minutes later he was knotting a tie at his throat—or trying to remember how to. She was probably expecting him to show up in jeans looking like a derelict.

The minx wasn't going to have it her own way. He'd told her he was coming after her, and he was. He did want to shake her up; he wanted to shake her out of that life-style rut she was in before she killed herself with overwork. He was not going to hurt her.

And whether the minx wanted it or not, she was not going to be rushed into bed.

He was going to be a perfect gentleman.

If it killed him.

Sitting on her back porch, wrapped in a bath towel, Kate sprayed her legs. White foam gushed from the can like marshmallows—menthol-smelling marshmallows. Dipping the pink-handled razor in a bowl of warm water, she glided the blade from her ankle to her knee, then shook off the foam.

It was 6:00 p.m., that time in the early evening when the wind hushed and the birds stopped singing and the sunlight looked all dusty. Upstairs on her uncle's feather bed lay a pair of filmy hose, a white lacy blouse and a black crepe skirt. Originally they'd been packed in the bottom of her suitcase; she always packed them there. All her life she'd believed in being prepared for all contingencies.

Mr. Kaufman had turned into a contingency.

When her legs were done, they felt sleek and cool and bare. She reached for her small cosmetic mirror and tweezers, angling both with the sun behind her. She plucked the first eyebrow and winced. Brooke Shields had brought natural eyebrows back "in." That was fine, but Kathryn never could stand stragglers. She plucked two more tiny hairs, wincing each time.

Why was she going through all these mating rituals for a man who might not even show up?

But he was going to show up. The knot in her stomach told her he was going to show up. She was tense as a cat.

When her legs and brows were done, she suffered an ice-cold outside shower, a pedicure and manicure, then pampered every inch of her skin with jasmine skin lotion. When that was dry, she slipped on a white lace bra and matching panties, then, sitting on the bed, she unraveled the silky hose. Before she dressed, she sprayed a layer of perfume on her body's heat spots.

Like a general planning a campaign, she fussed through every cosmetic she'd brought with her. First foundation, imperceptibly applied. The smallest hint of blush, a smudge of gold above her eyes, no more mascara than it took to darken her blond lashes. Then her hair. When she was completely finished, it was just after seven, and she'd accomplished exactly what she'd wanted to. The black pencil-slim skirt outlined her hips. The scent of jasmine followed her when she moved. Her white silk blouse buttoned in back and had a froth of lace at the wrists and a cutout from throat to bodice that revealed bare white skin to her bra line—the look was feminine and fragile, with a peek-a-boo tease, which was appropriate. Her make-up was flawless and heels gave her a leggy look. Gold dangled from her ears and throat.

She was ready to take on the United Nations.

Maybe not Grant.

Furthermore, she had an entire nervous hour to wait. Darn it, she'd planned on taking forever to dress. Why did she have to do everything so fast?

She settled at the kitchen table and opened a *Fortune* magazine she'd brought with her. Two minutes later an article on investments with double tax savings potential had all of her attention. Sort of.

At a quarter to eight she'd paced the room twenty-seven times and was standing in the doorway when she heard the sound of Grant's truck. Washed and waxed, it looked like someone else's. The man who stepped out of it also looked like a stranger.

His suit was light gray with a mild pinstripe; his tie could have been advertised in *Gentleman's Quarterly*. If she'd seen him on a street in Chicago, she would definitely have looked twice, although not necessarily done anything about it. His stride had purpose; his shoulders showed off power. A white shirt advertised his tan, and a Rolex watch glinted in the sunset when he pulled down his sleeve. Looking straight at her, he moved toward the porch steps.

The beard was gone. She knew the shape of his mouth, but had never seen it clearly before. His jawline was square, and he had the kind of chin that said no one with any sense would argue with him. She felt a terrible flutter of nerves as he took the last three steps toward the door.

It was a mistake to challenge him. It was a mistake to play games with a man who had played in bigger leagues than she ever had. It was a mistake to think she could ever affect this man's life as she'd planned to this night, to ever think she could teach him a lesson about freedom and responsibility. It was a mistake for her to care . . . and to ever think that she didn't.

"Hi."

She pushed open the door to let him in. "Hi," she murmured back, and felt his gaze drag over her top to toe until her nerves were jangling and her heart was thumping. Now, wait a minute, she thought. I know I look ready to be seduced. But see, I had this idiotic idea that you wouldn't. I had another idiotic idea that you cared more than you want to admit, that you wouldn't use me. And I had yet another idiotic idea that if I didn't trust my instincts this once, that the chance would be gone and I'd have lost something terribly important.

How could she explain? It was nothing she could say aloud. She said, "I can't believe how different you look without the beard."

He smiled, then leaned back against the wall, pure lazy Grant, one leg forward, hands on his hips. "Dammit, Kate, we're both dressed to beat the band with nowhere to go. And we've got a complication."

"What?"

"Baby."

"I don't see—" But there was a small cloud of dust following in the truck's wake. The bloodhound arrived, panting in the yard. Then she clumsily mounted the porch steps and groaned as she fell in a wrinkled heap against the door.

"She expects to go to dinner?" Kathryn said gravely.

"She's had dinner. She's just got this small problem with possessiveness," Grant said disgustedly.

"Well!" A sudden chuckle escaped from her. There was no way to hold tension with a bloodhound for a chaperon. Renewed courage laddered up the vertebrae in her spine. It was Grant, not a stranger in her cabin.

And it was time they had some fun.

"Will she stay in the back of the pickup if we take her?" Kathryn asked.

"We're not taking her."

Kathryn's eyes danced. "We'll buy her a bag of bones en route."

"No, Kate."

It was pitch-dark by the time they arrived at his destination. Kate had envisioned his taking her to the ratty little dive that sold catfish—where else could they go in this backwater?—but she'd dressed for Grant, not for wherever they were going.

She should have known he'd come up with the unexpected. As she stepped down from the truck, she could smell Lake Superior and feel its chill wrap around her. The lighthouse was tall and white, with an on-off beam of light splashing on the stone beach. A flurry of wind tossed her hair when she leaned over the back of the truck.

"Now, you stay," she told Baby sternly. A tail thumped wildly from the shadows of the truck bed.

Grant gave the dog a rueful look, then reached an arm behind Kate to guide her up the grassy knoll toward the lighthouse-restaurant. His hand, she noted, never actually touched her. Gentleman fashion, that hand of his had opened doors and made sure she was handed up and down from the pickup's high seat, but so far it hadn't made contact of any other kind. That same hand pulled out a chair for her a few minutes later when they were inside, without once brushing her shoulder or arm.

Later she would remember champagne and pickerel and the tang of a fine lemon sherbet, the dull gleam of silver and the sheen of linen. The lighthouse had three small floors, each circular and opening onto an open spiral staircase. Music floated up from the bottom floor, love songs murmuring from a piano so far away that they never quite seemed real. The window next to their table had a view of the lake, which was black, with ribbons of white fog skipping around foaming waves at the shore.

The place was enchanted by the lake and a man's black eyes, the privacy of a quiet room and the drug of champagne bubbles, distant love songs and Grant's smiles. An hour passed, maybe two. Dinner was long over and still they lingered at the table. Grant told stories of the sea, of pirates and shipwrecks on ice storm nights in winters past. He talked of minks and fur-trapping days and Michigan's gold rush. Who'd ever heard of Michigan's gold rush? He told her she looked beautiful and filled her champagne glass too many times. But he never once touched her.

Kathryn felt bemused and charmed and quiet. She'd never expected Grant's sophisticated side. All the rough edges were gone. His smoky-gray suit fit him as perfectly as his jeans and chamois shirts; he was capable of being elegantly mannered without losing any of his vital quality. She took a last sip of wine, well aware she was already light-headed. Recklessness was starting to tingle through her.

Leashed and controlled, Grant was a devastatingly attractive man. She could well picture him running his companies. She could too easily imagine him smoothly seducing a woman with wine and music. Unfortunately she missed her devil-eyed vagrant, and for a man who claimed he intended to pursue, he was suddenly being ridiculously cautious.

She noted Grant subtly motioning for the check. With surprise, she noted the flash of relief in Grant's eyes when the waiter brought the bill. He stood up. "Unfortunately, we still have minks that need tending to tonight." His tone was regretful.

And fake. "Dinner was wonderful," she said softly.

"We'll come again." She led the way down the circular stairs to the bottom floor, where the piano music was whispering through open windows and blending with the splash and rhythm of the lake's own love song.

"Do you dance?" she asked lightly. For the first time she noticed the pocket-sized parquet dance floor beside the pianist.

Grant steered her toward the door. "If I were a sadist, I'd answer yes. And luckily for you, the dance floor is crowded."

"It is," she agreed.

"And we have to get home."

"We do," she agreed again.

When he opened the outer door, he felt a wave of relief like he'd been through a war. He'd made it. He'd been a gentleman; he hadn't touched her. The scent of her perfume had nearly driven him mad; her eyes had turned seductively sleepy after that first glass of champagne; her cutout blouse had lured his gaze with hints of soft white breasts. And he hadn't once touched a hair on her head.

He was all but home free when her fingers suddenly laced in his. The grassy slope around the lighthouse had the sheen of velvet by night; a cool wind whipped off the lake, all mists and clouds and shadows.

"Come on," she said teasingly. "One dance, Grant—over there by the windows and the music. No one can see us. There's no light—"

"You'll be too cold."

"I won't be."

"It's already late—"

"Just one," she urged. "Just one dance."

But I can't risk touching you, Kathryn Price, he thought. "I have two left feet, Kate. I was telling you the truth about not being able to dance."

"I'll show you."

She teased him into the shadows, her lips glistening with soft laughter and coaxing teases. The splash and ripple of lake tide were far stronger than the wisp of a love song they could faintly hear from the piano. Dew soaked into her high-heeled sandals, and wind molded her frothy white blouse to her shape. He honestly couldn't dance.

Then she slid her arms around his waist under his suit coat and tucked her forehead against his cheek. Jasmine drowned him. Her hips cradled up to his and her sigh was like music. His arms slid around her neck. He couldn't help it.

"I have a confession to make," she whispered.

He tensed. "What?"

"I haven't been involved with a man since my ex-husband," she said softly. "You might have to do a little coaching."

"Coaching?" He couldn't imagine what she needed coaching in. She could have written a thesis on driving a man mad. Her hips alone knew rhythms far more potent than any love song.

"On making love," she murmured.

"Sweetheart . . ."

"I'm not worried," she whispered recklessly. "Not with you. With someone else...yes. But you've made it so clear you don't want anything long-term, and that's exactly what's so sweet. Freedom. All we have to think about is the here and now, what we feel, what we need." She gave a small, shy laugh. "You really will have to coach me a little. I'm not used to living for the moment, but I want to. I want to throw caution to the winds. Just once in my life. I've never done this . . ."

At his back, her fingers walked over his belt and strayed lower. She pressed on his hips.

"Or this . . ."

Her fingers climbed back out and moved over his jacket, shivered over his arms and shoulders, then whispered into his hair like an abandoned breeze.

"Or this . . ."

She applied the slightest pressure on his head and went up on tiptoe at the same time. Her breath teased his mouth, and then her lips pressed to his with the rub of sweet, wanton hunger. Her breasts crushed against his chest as if they'd found a warm bed after months of cold; her slim thighs layered against his. Until then he'd been making motions of following some kind of dance. He stopped trying.

He framed her face with his palms, then took again and again of her sweetness. She yielded like a flower to sun, opening up, vulnerable and soft. It could have started snowing for all he cared. He smelled night and sea wind; he tasted champagne and Kate. He felt a lady grow wild beneath his kisses, his touch, his answering hunger. God, he was lonely. For her.

She trembled, and he lifted his mouth. "Damn you, Kate," he whispered. "I'm not going to make love to you."

"Yes, you are."

"Not like this. Not with you thinking I don't give a damn. It was never like that. You misunderstood me."

"Did I?" she whispered. "Do you suddenly believe we have a future together?"

He hesitated. "I don't know."

"And you're completely happy alone, Grant. You have been for five years. Has that changed?"

"No, but—"

"Then it's this or nothing, yes?" Her eyes were a silky blue by moonlight, her lips still damp from his kisses. "I wasn't arguing with you. Don't you understand? I'm willing to take what you offered. No more, no less. No demands. Isn't that what you wanted?"

"Yes. No!" He'd desperately wanted to see Kathryn loosen up, but while *he* was in control. He wanted her to avoid making the mistakes he'd made. He saw a need in Kate and wanted to be that someone who filled it. "Kate, I don't want to hurt you," he said gruffly.

"That's my risk to take, not yours," she whispered. "Take me home?"

On the ride back in the darkness, she eased her head against his shoulder, eyes closed, relaxed in a way she couldn't ever remember being before. This was right...she increasingly knew that every time he touched her. She felt alive when she was with him, vibrantly, stingingly alive. Loving him couldn't be wrong.

Decisions gelled that had been eluding her for weeks. She hadn't needed Grant to tell her she should change her life. She couldn't live forever in a cage any more than her minks could. Freedom meant risk, an end to emotional safety. She was ready to take that risk, to reach out for a new balance in her life. None of that was *for* Grant, but she hoped she could do it with him.

He needed it, too, she thought fleetingly. He belonged back in the civilized world...and it would happen. She'd help him see that compromise didn't mean losing but changing.

Grant drove into his yard less than an hour later, cast a glance at the sleeping lady nestled against his shoulder and sighed. Silently opening the truck door, he climbed out and pushed down the tailgate as quietly as possible. Baby didn't want to move. She was too happy with the five dollars' worth of dog bones Kate had bought, and had stuffed them into one corner.

"Now!" he commanded.

Baby licked his hand but didn't move.

"All right, stay there then," Grant whispered irritably, and stalked over to the passenger side of the truck.

Kate had gained weight, for which he took all the credit—he'd been supplying her breakfasts and lunches—and for which he now seemed to be suffering all the penalties. Also, when she slept, she *slept*. Not needing to turn on lights, he carried her through to his bed in the far room, disposed of her shoes and black crepe skirt and covered her with a quilt.

Then he stared at her as he stripped off every ounce of civilized male attire and reluctantly tugged jeans and a sweatshirt back on. In the best of worlds, he'd be sleeping next to her. In the worst, he had to be out for the next few hours guarding her mink.

Now it was the worst of worlds. Fifteen minutes later, a shotgun held under one arm, he was walking the uneven ground near their mink pens. Clouds rolled past a bone-white moon. With any luck, it would rain all night tomorrow. Tonight, shadows streaked with shadows... he saw deer, fox, two muskrat. He heard an owl and the rare, mournful howl of a distant wolf. During the day, mink had few natural predators. Midnight was their dangerous time, their vulnerable time.

His vulnerable time.

He breathed in the night air, the solitude, the smells of forest and night. Everything he valued was here. Survival wasn't easy, but it was honest. Nature never lied. He could remember a paper-filled office and a phone constantly ringing; he could remember the smells of an overflowing ashtray and stale coffee and the sounds of constant noise. He'd once consumed problems like nectar, once loved the world of business, and yes, he missed it. The challenge of surviving off the land had sustained him in the beginning. Lately he'd been missing the other world more.

But he wasn't going back. For one thing, it was too late now, too much time had passed. For another, he'd always been an all or nothing man. He'd never be able to return halfway. He knew himself.

He also had a problem. Belatedly it occurred to him that without thinking he'd taken Kate home—to his home, his bed. The instinct had been an unconscious one. She belonged with him. She'd also brought him darn close to an explosion on a dark wet lawn as they'd danced to the waltz of the sea. It was what he wanted for her—to feel free to be impulsive, foolish, alive, whatever she really was at her core.

He wanted her with a craving, an obsession—but not if he had to give up his freedom to have her.

She wasn't really awake. Predawn fuzziness still coated the room in shadows. Dreams still lingered under her half-closed eyelids. In one dream, the mattress dipped next to her.

Grant's body was cool and bare. Silent and slow as a cat, he leaned over her to tuck the covers under her chin, and then lay back. His hair was rumpled, and his eyes looked hollow and exhausted. He stiffened when he felt her arm slide across his chest.

"You've been out all night with the minks?" she whispered. "You should have woken me."

His eyes were closed. He still smiled. "Honey, when you crash, an army could walk over your stomach and you'd never know." He added, "Go back to sleep. It's still early."

"Did we lose any?"

"None. They're all safe, Kate. Don't worry."

"You're cold."

"I'm fine. Go to sleep." Weariness echoed in the hoarseness of his voice.

He turned on his side, away from her. She turned with him, feeling his cold seep into her sleep-warm body as she wrapped herself around him. Her nipples tightened against his chilled spine, and goose bumps rose on her bare legs where they tucked under his.

"Kate—"

"Hush." It was an order. She'd always been good at giving orders and arranging things. It took a moment before she had everything settled to her satisfaction—the quilt nestled under his chin, her arm curved across his ribs and the drape of her body positioned to give him maximum warmth. Then she snuggled her cheek near his shoulder and closed her eyes again, waiting for him to relax and sleep.

It took him a long time, long enough that a smile gradually curved into her cheeks. He wasn't used to a woman's protective touch. He wasn't used to anyone taking care of him. A wash of love filled her. The vibrations should have been sexual—he was bare and she was nearly so, and certainly the touch of him had never failed to arouse her. She felt aroused now, too, but with different emotions.

Like a wild creature, he seemed to run from care. He took it for granted that he had to depend on himself. He expected nothing from anyone; he was afraid of needing anyone. And she understood those things so well because they were all feelings she'd shared— before she'd met him.

One couldn't tame a wild creature overnight.

She slept, dreaming about beginnings.

Seven

Lightning slashed the sky as Kathryn pulled into Grant's driveway. She grabbed the large white box and bag from the seat as the first fat drops of rain plopped on the truck's windshield. The sky looked like a charcoal wasteland, bleak and dark even though it was only six o'clock. By the time she threw a jacket over her head and raced for the door, raindrops had turned into millions of needles.

Gasping, she pulled open Grant's door. It was hushed and gloomy inside. She glanced toward the red blanket curtaining Grant's bed, but there was no movement. Using one heel to push into the other, she slipped off her shoes. Then, still holding the bag and box, she dropped her jacket on a hook.

Tiptoeing toward his cupboards, she foraged silently for glasses and silverware. Baby appeared out of nowhere, her tail thumping louder than the thunder outside.

"Sssh," Kathryn whispered.

The tail thumped harder.

"Do you want to go out?" she whispered.

More thumps.

"No, you smell food. I should have known. Well, where's your dish, darn it?" But she could see the shadow of a dog's dish in the corner, adequately filled. Dog food obviously couldn't compete with the smell of pizza. Trying to ignore Baby's mournful eyes, Kathryn searched for a tray and then tiptoed across the room for the lantern on the mantel. Lifting the glass cover, she reached into her jeans pocket for matches.

Lit, the lantern gave the room a soft glow, softening stone and putting a sheen on wood. Still, one fierce clap of thunder made her shiver. The storm was wild, deliciously so. Outside, willows and poplars bent under a fierce wind; maple and oak branches shook. She fleetingly thought that it was typical of these north woods: it couldn't simply rain; it had to be a deluge.

Still tiptoeing, she carried the tray to Grant's corner, pushed aside his dividing curtain and abruptly raised her eyes to the ceiling. "I was trying to be so quiet. I thought you were still sleeping!"

"I was. What's this?"

Grant eased up to a sitting position, propping the pillows behind him. He'd slept like the dead after being up all night, and still felt drugged...but not so

drugged that he hadn't immediately woken at the
sound of a soft footstep and the smell of jasmine. She
was wearing a black-and-white striped blouse tucked
into black jeans with a scarf for a belt. She made him
think of female pirates and trouble. In fact, she was
already wagging a managerial finger at him.

"No complaints," she warned as she set the tray on
his lap. "I never claimed to be a cook to begin with,
and anything I'd have made at my cabin would have
been cold before I got it here. I looked in your freezer,
but that didn't help. I've never even had venison . . . so it's take-out pizza and Coke or nothing."

"Stop apologizing. Pizza sounds terrific."

"It isn't." She felt miserable. "When I think of the
blueberry pancakes you made me—"

He motioned her down to the bed beside him. "The
point is that we promote good habits."

"Habits?"

"The habit of having our meals in bed."

Bold eyes met hers until she felt heat flame in her
cheeks. In his sleep he'd been marvelously docile. Last
night, for that matter, he'd specialized in charm and
distance. Those gloves were off. The quilt barely covered his hair-splattered chest; the hair on his head was
rumpled. Desire snapped in his eyes, and so did a
primitive satisfaction—she was here, on his bed, where
he wanted her. If there were more complex emotions
involved between them, his smile indicated they were
of no immediate importance.

Sitting on one leg, she cut a slice for him. Cheese
predictably stretched like a rubber band when she

lifted it to a plate. She licked a finger and felt his eyes follow the trail of her tongue. Whatever zinged through her veins, it wasn't blood. She had to struggle to find simple conversation. "You think the minks will be all right in the storm?"

"They won't like the wet any more than their predators will, but they'll be safe for the night. What did you do all day?"

"Wallpapered. Curtained. Scraped and painted the iron bedstead up in my uncle's loft. And I went into town to call home."

"And?" Her busy day didn't surprise him until she'd tacked on the last comment. His eyes narrowed uneasily as he took in her expression.

She hesitated, half mesmerized by watching him eat. Consuming pizza was never a delicate process. She inevitably tore off small bites and propped up stragglers of cheese so that they didn't have a chance to dangle. Not Grant. He ate like he did everything else—with earthy, lusty pleasure. His teeth tore into the crust; his tongue savored the cheese strings. There was no mess because it was all devoured.

"I have to go home," she said quietly. He stopped eating and looked at her. "Not for long," she said swiftly, "but I'd only originally planned being gone two weeks. I have to arrange things differently if I'm going to be away longer, and I'd hoped to do that by telephone, but it just won't work. The day after tomorrow is Thursday. If I drive down to Chicago then, I should be able to do everything I have to in two days. I'd be back on Sunday." She drew a breath. "I'm sorry. I seem to have to ask for your help again. It isn't fair to leave you with the responsibility for the minks, but—"

"I'll watch your damn minks," he said shortly. Never mind all his hesitations about being involved with her, all he could think of at the moment was that if she left now, she might not come back. She'd come a long way if she could comfortably eat pizza while sitting barefoot on his bed. She was wearing her hair more loosely now, too, not all cramped up with pins the way it had been when she'd first arrived.

"What's wrong?" she asked.

"Nothing." Everything.

Her eyes danced. "Pizza isn't exactly the best of foods for breakfast."

"It's fine, Kate." But her leaving wasn't. He thought about her going back, instantly immersing herself in the rat race again, forgetting to eat, forgetting to sleep, maybe wanting to forget that for a few short days she'd nearly slept with a man who had offered her nothing more than emotions and an illusion of freedom. Perhaps there was even a man in her life in Chicago, someone whom she'd been hesitating about being involved with...there had to be men in her life. Even if Kate were reticent, Chicago men couldn't all be blind.

He thought of how far she'd come in just a few short weeks. The lady was learning to take risks, and now dared to dance in the darkness. Even a week before, she would have squashed the impulse, afraid of looking foolish. Last night he'd been disastrously aware of the web Kate was weaving around him. It didn't matter. He wanted her free to be foolish. With him. Foolish and impulsive, her laughter like wind...

"Can I?" she asked.

"Can you what?"

Her empty plate back on the tray, she was petting Baby, whose head was a deadweight on her knee. "I can't stand her sorrowful eyes. Can I feed her a piece of pizza?"

"After the royal pain she was last night? You have to be kidding." He rubbed his hands on a napkin, then moved the tray to the bedside table.

Baby longingly stared at the last piece of pizza. Kate deliberately stood up, just out of Grant's reach. "We're going to ignore your master," she informed the dog. "Just because he's a grouchy old bear when he wakes up is no excuse for you to suffer."

The bloodhound had barely taken off with the booty before Kathryn felt two hands capture her waist from behind. He ignored her screech of laughter and wrestled her to the mattress in a confusion of limbs. Pinned with both arms above her head and his blanketed leg draped over her, he suggested, "Want to tell me again what a grouchy old bear I am?"

"Well, you are. Did I get one thank-you for bringing your breakfast?"

"Dinner," he corrected.

"Well, dinner then. And if you tickle me again, I won't be responsible for my knee."

"I'll be responsible for your knee. And I was getting around to my thank-you. You never gave me a chance. First, are you going to call me a grouchy old bear again?''

"Honestly, Grant. I mean, when the shoe fits, the shoe fits."

"And are you going to continue to cater to that worthless wastrel of a spoiled mutt?''

"At every opportunity."

He shook his head in despair. "Ah, Kate. You leave me no choice."

Her lips were curved in laughter, and every limb stiffened to spring away from his tickling fingers. She was prepared for nonsense, not for his mouth slowly dropping onto hers. In the pulse of a second, her world changed colors. Time suspended in his eyes.

"Grant—"

"Hush. I'm busy thanking you for breakfast."

He wasn't thanking her for breakfast; he was kissing her senseless. He tasted like spice, and his lips were warm. Somewhere a dog moaned at a rolling echo of thunder. It seemed so dark, not like late afternoon but like midnight. All she could hear was the rain pelting on the windows, a storm lashing at the door that couldn't get in.

Grant was everywhere. The taste of him spun in her head. His mouth wooed and ravished, gave and took, demanded and so generously crushed hers. She'd anticipated the weight of him in her imagination. She'd guessed he wouldn't be a patient lover, but wild and bold and dangerously sensual. Still, she wasn't prepared. In time, or sometime, or soon, she always knew it would come to this, but not at dinner, not during an afternoon, not . . . so consumingly fast.

Last night she'd gotten lost in darkness. The game had been to arouse him, yes, and she'd desperately hoped to tease him into caring, but something had gone wrong. She hadn't cared how or why or what he'd felt; she had only wanted him to keep holding her. Last night she'd succumbed to a fantasy of sweet foolishness, and now . . .

There was no fantasy. Just a man, and a storm, the feel of her blouse buttons being loosened one by one, the feel of his lips and whiskered chin whispering over her bare throat. She shivered suddenly, violently.

Yes. Her fingers caressed his smooth, bare shoulders, not wanting to let go. She wanted to unravel the dark curling hair on his chest. She wanted to feel the muscles of his hips tighten because of her. She wanted to know Grant. She'd wanted to know him from the minute she'd met him.

Yes. His tongue stoked the heat of hers. She heard his breathing change, felt his black eyes open on her eyes. She understood at once that he wouldn't have pressed her to continue, only that he *wanted* her to. And then he ducked his head. Two fingers unsnapped the front clasp of her bra, and then he was buttoning her bare chest with kisses from throat to navel. Restless . . . she'd been restless all her life, but not like this, not like a tantrum of urgency when his tongue painted one breast hot and wet and so damned tight.

Yes. Her blood whispered, "Yield." Her heart pounded with it. It had to be right. She'd never known desire as this man made her feel it, never ached like this man made her ache. To be taken ... no. To be seduced ... no. She had a right to reach out, a right to give. For the rest of her life she'd be good again, careful and cautious. For this moment, she had a man to claim as hers, to possess as hers, to love him whether or not he wanted to be loved.

She pushed aside his blanket. It was in the way. Her fingers stroked and rubbed. Her lips teased and took. She slid her jeans-clad leg against his bare thigh and let the tips of her breasts drag against his chest. She felt him tighten, harden, tense against her.

The rain just wouldn't stop. She heard it battering against the windows, sensed a distant flickering of light, shivered at the howl of lonely wind. Not here. Here there was a man who touched her with hunger, a man whose skin grew slick with need, a man who tasted like desire and sounded like a man fighting for breath. Driving him mad took all her attention. She wanted to love him until he shattered. She wanted to give as she'd never understood giving, just ... free. Herself. A woman. Not Kathryn, but his Kate. Only something went wrong, because his Kate suddenly needed something so desperately.

Grant eased the jeans from her hips without ever losing his seal on her mouth. Wonder softened his touch, controlled the aggressive, dominant need to take her inside of him. He'd guessed at Kate's passion, sampled its fringes, but had never fathomed the depths of the complex woman she was. She was a wanton, greedy for pleasure, exulting in the lightest touch. She was shy, believing herself bold, even though her gentle, intimate forays told him how little experience she'd really had. She was abandoned, high on freedom, sassy and exhilarated with her own feminine powers.

And she was suddenly shaken. Trembling. Vulnerable. Kate. As far as he could tell, she was doing everything in her power to be taken with the force and delicacy of a freight train.

She wasn't going to get what she wanted.

The scrap of panties had to go. He made silk with his tongue, on her thigh, on her abdomen, on her throat. He touched with tenderness. He touched with love. And he whispered to her. Her cheeks flushed so he whispered more.

The lady was willing, and his body was tense and hurting with the need for release. He held off. He needed to please Kate; it wasn't a choice. He wanted her to need him, to be the one to make her soar. He wanted every inch of her skin branded his, branded with tender heat and gentleness, and those wants simply grew, those needs kept exploding.

He covered her. When he slid inside her, the moment became engraved in his mind. She was tight, and moist, and her legs wrapped around him. Her skin had a golden sheen, her eyes were glazed, and her breath was shallow with strain. "Come to me," she whispered. "Come to me, Grant . . . Now. Fast . . ."

It was not how she understood lovemaking, to let go . . . everything. It was not how she understood life. One protected oneself with inhibitions. She felt none.

Every part of him belonged to her, not just skin and muscle and bone, but his fierceness, his passion, his loneliness. His rhythm was her rhythm, his need her need.

Lightning flashed inside her, brilliant, sharp, breathtaking, rippling through her again and again. Grant's hoarse cry echoed her own.

The rain kept falling. Grant shifted, easing his weight off her and closing his eyes. He appeared to be catnapping, but when she tried to free herself from his arms, he tightened his hold. "Stay there," he ordered huskily.

She'd never been good at following orders. Persisting, she finally escaped his grasp so that she could angle upward to rest on an elbow. His arm immediately closed possessively on her hip. A smile curved her lips. Her body was still tingling, her heart still reeling from the depth of emotional release she'd just shared with him. A textbook might have labeled her feelings "sexual satisfaction" and explained her rocketing glow as something any woman might feel after a long period of sexual deprivation.

Textbooks didn't know anything.

Neither did she, except that she was simultaneously shaken up and filled with lazy well-being. She was old enough to know that no one built love through sex, but trust was an integral ingredient to good lovemaking. A woman was vulnerable, bare. And when a woman made love, she was at her most easily hurt, mentally, physically and emotionally. Without trust in her mate, it simply couldn't be good.

Grant hadn't just given her good lovemaking; he'd made the sky explode, which told her exactly how much trust she'd given him, and how preciously he'd treated her trust.

She pushed back the tousled hair on his forehead, touched his cheek, his chin. She kissed his nose. That made his eyes open. He couldn't have been sleeping too soundly if he could instantly waken with an expression of sheer, dominant male possessiveness.

Taming the beast, she thought wryly, could turn into an all-consuming project. Shaving off his beard really hadn't helped. He still looked half savage and his black eyes still shone like fire. He would undoubtedly like the thought that he looked cold and dangerous. Unimpressed, she stroked his cheek again and bent down to kiss danger. "I have never," she said softly, "felt anything like that in my life."

"Neither have I." Tension faded when he understood she wasn't trying to withdraw from him. Amusement softened his eyes. He was still half dead, but Kate was vibrating with renewed energy. "You wouldn't like to tuck up close for a little nap?"

"No." She was too busy touching his throat, kissing his forehead. The rainbow would have to fade; she'd have to worry about them and what could and couldn't be, but not yet. "Do you feel like doing cartwheels?"

"God, no."

"Climbing mountains? Walking on water?"

"If you're not careful, you're going to give me the definite impression that you're happy."

"I am. Crazy happy. You're a beautiful man, Kaufman. You terrify me. There are definitely moments when I could shoot you, but not now. Where the heck were you when I was a virgin and desperately needed you?"

His mouth twisted into a devilish grin. She made it sound as if he'd been irresponsible and lax for not being in her life at the time. "I'll bet you were a tease."

"That's half the fun of being seventeen," she informed him. "Besides, I've changed."

"I noticed that. Do you know what your left hand is doing?"

She glanced down. "Heavens."

"I'm afraid I'm down for at least a fifteen-minute count, honey. You're dreaming if you think you can get blood out of a turnip."

"I have news for you. That's no turnip."

His throaty chuckle filled their dark private corner. She stretched languidly, and then thumped his chest with her forefinger. "I have a terrible problem," she confessed.

"What?"

"Starvation."

He shook his head. "You can't be hungry. You just finished nearly half a pizza."

"I can't help that."

"Well...how does a venison steak sound?"

"Too filling."

"A slice of prairie bread?"

"That sounds fascinating, but no. I need . . ." She hesitated, and then sat up. The craving hit her like lust. "Sweet cherries."

"Sorry," he said regretfully. "I picked a bowlful but they're gone."

"There's a tree close by?"

Jets should be so fast. Her pert hips were swinging across the room before he could stop her. She found his red chamois shirt hanging on a hook. "Kate," he said patiently, "it's raining."

"Yes, but luckily the thunder and lightning's stopped."

"It's also dark."

"It usually is when the sun goes down." His shirt wouldn't make a bad dress if she had a belt. It was soft, and had the current loose look the fashion pages favored. But the first throat button hit her midchest, and she exposed Grant to a full view when she leaned over to kiss the top of his head. "You just stay right here and relax. You don't mind if I borrow one of your jackets, do you? And I'll take Baby. We won't be more than a few minutes. . . ."

He already knew she wasn't going to be more than a few minutes, because he was going with her. Three steps out the door, and they were both soaked. The storm had settled down to a steady downpour, and Kathryn seemed determined to dance through it. His jacket dragged on her like a bag lady's, her hair fell in straggly wet ringlets and her bare legs disappeared inside the sprawling old cherry tree with abandoned ease.

"Kate, you're nuts!"

"I know, and this worries me. Seriously worries me. Would you hand up the bowl?" He saw her face as she peeked through wet branches. "I'm not given to impulse, you know. I'm never given to impulse—oh, God!"

Her teeth squished into the sweet red fruit. She closed her eyes and smelled rain and pines and grass and cherries.

"What's wrong?" Grant asked with alarm.

"They're so good!"

He grinned in the darkness.

"You know how many cherry trees they grow in Chicago?"

He felt like the setup man for a comedian. "How many?"

"None. Here." She handed him down a full bowl, and with a mouthful of cherries, climbed back down. Her grin was exultant, and she spread her arms like a scarecrow. "Will you look at this? Rain!"

"It rains in Chicago."

"Not like this. It rains gray in Chicago. Here it makes everything smell good and look soft, and it even tastes good!"

He had to reach for her. This was the Kate he wanted for her, lighthearted and carefree and nothing more complicated than happy. Her cherries were spilling to the ground.

He molded his lips to hers. Rain dripped from her lashes, splashing on skin that was already impossibly soft. She tasted sweet and tangy...and sticky. Her fingers were stickier yet when they reached up and encircled his neck, climbing into his hair. He licked the cherry juice off her cheeks, then homed in on her mouth again.

With who else, her heart kept murmuring, with who else could she be this silly, this foolish, this happy, this... free? Nothing else mattered but loving him.

Grant never lost total control. Every instinct demanded he get her back inside, warm and dry and safe. The rain was madness, and so was Kate. She flowed in and around him, too willing, too sweet, all heat-giving fire. She wouldn't listen. The grass was wet and cold and springy, and laughter whispered into that night, then silence.

"I told you about Ranker and the rent." Bess finished the last forkful of take-out Chinese and refolded the lid on the little white box.

"Yes. I'm going to see him for lunch tomorrow." In high heels and a lime-green suit, Kathryn crossed to her ivory counter and poured a cup of coffee—possibly her ninetieth in the past twenty-four hours. She'd been in Chicago twenty-four hours.

Old habits easily reasserted themselves. Her stomach was sloshing with caffeine, her feet hurt and her temples pounded with a devilish headache. Friday had been stuffed with banking, display windows, quarterly tax reports, customers, receipts... and decisions. When the store had closed at nine, she'd moved Bess and Chinese food to her apartment. The work day wasn't over yet. "You've managed beautifully," she complimented Bess.

The brunette flushed with pleasure. Bess's dress was jewel-red, and the scarf at her throat was tied with a saucy flair. "You didn't think I could?"

"I knew you could," Kathryn corrected, "but I also knew it wasn't fair to leave that much work for you to do alone. I called the employment agency. They're sending over two extras on Monday." Her head was filled with tomorrow's activities. She had a rent battle on her hands and a meeting with her CPA. Spring receipts had to be tabulated against the influx of capital needed to put fall clothes on the racks. Her minks seemed a continent away, and Grant desperately too far. She'd been doing her best not to think of him. She couldn't.

"Kathryn?"

She glanced up, affectionately watching her assistant clasp her hands in her lap. Kathryn knew what was coming, and this too had to be tactfully handled now.

"I hope you haven't forgotten," Bess said hesitantly. "You said you'd think about a partnership, and that the next time we had a free minute to talk..." She drew a breath. "I hoped you would see what I could handle while you were gone."

"I have," Kathryn said smoothly. Carefully she set down the porcelain cup. She'd seen exactly what Bess wanted her to see—that her assistant had drive, determination, pride, ambition, capability. The subject of a partnership had come up before. "I've thought about it a great deal."

Kathryn had always squelched the idea—gently, of course—on the grounds that Bess was too young, too untried, not tough enough to share the equal responsibilities involved in a partnership. In many ways that was still true—but she'd never faced the strongest reason she'd refused to consider it. The store had been her baby and no one else's for so long. Everything had been her risks, her triumphs, her fears, her mistakes.

"All right." Bess, interpreting her silence as defeat, stood up and reached for her purse. "I didn't think you'd change your mind."

"I didn't say that." Efficiently Kathryn whisked the paperwork on the coffee table into her briefcase. "I still don't know how long I'm going to be up north, but when I get back, we'll see an attorney. I've already talked to one today about incorporating. Stock's the only way to do it, Bess. That way you can buy in as you feel you can financially afford to. We'll set up a legal arrangement so that you can ultimately buy in for a full half—but not at once. I'm not about to let you put your entire life in hock even if you could come up with the capital. I also refuse to encourage you to take the responsibility of a full partnership too fast. We'll set up an insurance package to protect you from any unfair proportion of liabilities. Then, if you change your mind—"

From the stranglehold Bess had around her neck, Kathryn doubted her assistant had any intention of changing her mind. The two shared a hug and laughter... and another half hour of serious talk before Kathryn claimed exhaustion and insisted Bess go home.

Alone then, she locked up, kicked off her lime leather pumps and sighed. The decision had come hard, and she wasn't totally at ease with it. She could have chosen to find a silent partner—an older, more experienced person in retail. Bess *was* too young, but she wouldn't always be. Her love of and commitment to the store were there. That mattered more than anything to Kathryn, and soon relief flooded her like a soothing balm.

It was done. She'd acted instead of just talked about making a very real change in her life to get off the responsibility treadmill.

Padding barefoot, she started switching off lights. For the first time in a long time, she really noticed her apartment—the peach-colored couch, the film of peach draperies, the touches of ivory in the living room. Her toes sank into the soft shag carpet. Her bedroom was decorated in more pastels and smelled like jasmine. The oil painting over her bed was her pride and joy—a surrealistic blend of rich cream, peach and green that perhaps no one else could possibly like. She loved it.

She loved all of it. By the time she'd undressed and slid into cool percale sheets, she'd rediscovered that she loved everything she had. Not only did the place belong to her, it was her. She liked to come home to pastels, comfort and soft textures. She liked sleek contemporary lines where she worked and feminine softness where she lived.

Nothing had changed. Outhouses weren't her style. Dripping sweat under a sweltering sun and carrying mink cages was something to be lived through, not enjoyed. She'd choose cream carpet over mosquitoes any day.

Only everything had changed. No matter how thoroughly she'd immersed herself in work over the past twenty-four hours, she couldn't get her mind off sweet cherries—and a man whose life-style she simply couldn't live with.

She fluffed and refluffed her pillow. The bed was lonely, empty, cold. Any fool should be able to sleep after the day she'd put in.

Only a fool would make love in the pouring rain in the dark under a cherry tree.

She loved Grant. She desperately missed him, but dreams of happy endings were elusive. She'd needed to learn balance in her life. A partnership with Bess was a beginning, a way to climb out of the tangle of responsibilities. She'd done that for her, not for Grant, and she'd done it to have the chance to face what really mattered to her.

Grant mattered to her, so much, too much—and she couldn't sleep, all too aware he'd never promised a future. From the beginning, he'd never believed they had one.

Eight

A shotgun rested on Grant's knee, and a thermos of coffee sat beside him. It was two in the morning on Sunday. From the crest of the knoll, he had a good view of the mink pens. Above him, he caught glimpses of a star-studded sky and a white cradle moon through the tree branches. He also saw the shadow of a hoot owl. The owl knew he was there and had visions of mink for dinner as soon as Grant left the territory.

He took another sip of coffee. His gaze traveled again through shadows and silver-lit clearings. The minks were out and active. He saw one, a caramel topaz, spray the area all around the rock where Grant had earlier hidden her food. She pounced on the raw meat and took off with it, happy as a thief.

Faster than he'd ever expected, they'd taken to being in the wild again. They hadn't had to learn to hunt live prey yet, but that was next. Their natural instincts had to be honed first—instincts of caution and defense. He'd worked with wild animals before, but never quite like this. They were all beautiful, the sheen of their fur lustrous and incomparably soft by moonlight. They were all sassy—high on freedom, too blithely assuming their safety. They shivered all over when a predator neared, not with fear, but with I-dare-you excitement.

They made him think of Kate. Soft. Sassy. Give her a taste of freedom and she soared. It was a bigger world than she thought, and one inhabited with a different breed of predator than the world she'd lived in before.

Like him.

He hadn't missed her. Everything had been nice, peaceful and quiet without her. Her Chicago trip was a hint of things to come. She'd leave again, but next time it would be for good. To get all wrapped up in caring about her was crazy. Feeling guilty for taking what she freely offered was equally crazy.

She shook everything up and upset him. For three long nights he'd convinced himself it would be easier all the way around if she didn't come back. Then he'd catch himself remembering making love in the pouring rain and feel tied up in knots again.

It was so quiet he could hear the rustle of a leaf. The first crunch of branch near the creek bed, and he forgot Kate. Flicking the safety off the shotgun, he hunched forward. Brush hid his view, but another twig snapped. Silently he raised the gun to his shoulder. The sounds were too heavy for a muskrat, and a fox was never that careless. He expected a deer. Deer didn't prey on mink, but a rare wolf still roamed these parts, and so did bobcats. Both were night creatures.

Neither, however, wore red silk blouses and a curl of upswept corn silk for a hairstyle—or skulked around the underbrush like a boy playing cowboys and Indians. He saw the gleam of long metallic black and instantly lurched to his feet. The crazy woman was armed.

His heart was suddenly racing like a roller coaster. Dammit. It had taken long enough for her to get here.

Ten yards ahead of Kate, something plopped in the water, nearly scaring her out of her wits. After driving all day, her first thought had been to crash for a good eight hours in her uncle's loft...except that Grant had been left tending the minks for the past three nights. It was time she did her share.

The principle was fine until she'd actually gotten out in the darkness. The idea of these night shifts was to protect the mink from predators. This implied they had real ones. Visions of circling wolves and slithery snakes darted in her head. She'd never once asked about snakes, and every moonlit black twig looked exactly like a reptile.

Something slimy jerked on the rock just ahead of her. Instantly she raised the gun and shot...and had the gun lifted out of her hands so fast that her heart completely stopped.

"I think you got him," Grant said gravely.

"Got what?"

"The frog."

"I thought it was a snake!" Her pulse stopped pumping adrenaline the minute she recognized Grant's tall dark form. It started pumping something else instead. His black eyes glanced at her gun, then with lazy, familiar amusement back at her. She could have sworn she smelled cherries.

"Snakes are all curled up under a nice warm rock at this time of night, honey." He clicked on the safety of his shotgun.

"Well, then, a bear."

Grant nodded. "You were going to take out a bear with a kid's popgun? A new purchase, I take it?"

"Well, I didn't want a real gun, just something to make noise. I mean, the point was never to hurt anything, just to scare off their predators—never mind. Wipe that grin off your face and give me a hug, Grant."

Giving orders, and she hadn't been back two minutes. Never mind how much he hadn't missed her. He enfolded her in his arms and smelled jasmine. It didn't take one good crush before he realized she wasn't wearing a bra beneath her blouse, or that the fragile shadows of tiredness made her eyes look huge—he knew he shouldn't have let her go back to Chicago. He kissed her and tasted sweet, yielding madness.

Her eyes searched his for a moment. His kiss had been rough, swift, possessive. Angry? Because she left or because she'd come back? But then he tucked both guns under one arm and draped an arm around her shoulder with the other.

"For heaven's sake, start talking," she said impatiently. "I have a thousand questions for you—how our babies have been doing, how you've been doing, where's Baby, what you've been up to—"

"Baby's at your side, waiting patiently for you to pet her."

"Oh." With a grin, she reached down to hug the tail-thumping bloodhound.

"I've been trapping live prey for our varmints...collected every cage from every hunter from here to Poughkeepsie. We've almost enough to get the minks started hunting. Pack rats and field mice, fish, a few rabbit..."

Slowly they circled the pens, which wasn't a short walk. They raised enough noise—and human scent— to send the minks skittering for cover, but every once in a while Kathryn caught a glimpse of moonlight-silver fur, lush, rich and soft. At the far end of the property, though, she noticed rolled-up wire fencing—the loss of three pens, four? She raised stricken eyes to Grant.

He took a breath. "We lost five," he said quietly. "Wolverine. Don't get upset. I warned you from the beginning that we'd inevitably suffer some loss. As fast as we can catch live prey and get the minks hunting naturally, the less we'll lose because that means we'll be closer to setting them free altogether. Kate?"

She knelt down beside Baby, letting her fingers get lost in all that wrinkled fur. A wet tongue washed her cheek. She smiled. "I'm not upset. Why would I be upset? Mangy varmints. And they're vicious. Mean. It's not like a person could ever get attached to them."

Grant crouched. He knew that lighthearted tone of voice. She used it whenever she was hurting. His palm stole up to her nape and rubbed soothingly. "In a cage," he said slowly, "they would have survived. They would have been fed and controlled and kept clean and warm...and their whole life would have been bars. They would never know fear or cold, Kate, but they would also never have been free. Freedom carries risk. There's nothing sentimental about it."

"I know that," she said sharply. "But that last cage...I remember, she was a mother, Grant. She had two young."

He took another breath, noticing the sheen of tears in her eyes. "We can drop the whole damn thing. Put them back in cages."

"No." She'd suddenly understood the measure of power she'd taken. In choosing to free the minks, she'd put them at risk. She'd rationally known that before, but not emotionally. She'd wanted to do something good; she'd never wanted the power to hurt anything or anyone.

Grant's palm touched her cheek. "We'll push them, Kate, as fast as we can. As of tomorrow, we'll start offering them their natural live food. They'll hunt or go hungry, and they'll learn damn fast because it's their nature to want to survive."

But the risks would also increase, she thought fleetingly, then straightened. "Never mind me," she said wryly. "I'm just having a rare emotional fit. I'll get over it."

A grin cut into his cheeks, then faded. "It's not easy," he said gently. "Making choices is never easy, Kate. You have to choose what you value and you have to do it every day."

"Darn it, is it really so easy for you? Don't you ever doubt? You would so easily and always choose freedom?" she demanded.

Her sudden fire startled him, but he couldn't lie. "Always." There was no other answer he could give her, but when she stalked off, he dragged a hand through his hair. For that instant her eyes had been dark sparklers. Her shoulders had squared like a duchess's.

He'd thought they were talking about the minks.

A week later Kathryn was sitting in his truck, the heated engine idling and competing with a hot, humid afternoon. Grant appeared from a clearing, wearing gloves and carrying two wire cages covered with netting. He plopped them in the truck bed, pushed up the tailgate and vaulted into the passenger side. She shifted immediately into reverse.

"What'd you catch this time?" she asked.

"Field mice in the one cage. We've got more than four dozen now."

"So last on the list is a stop for the fish?"

"Yes." He tossed her a glance. "Stop gritting your teeth, Kate."

"I just think life would be a whole lot nicer if we all ate leaves," she said dryly. Grant chuckled, leaning back. All week the two of them had been "salting" the mink pens with live prey. Technically the minks had it easy with such captive prey, but they still had to stalk and kill—or go hungry. The minks had caught on fast. Kathryn's stomach wasn't recovering nearly as quickly.

"We'll be home in an hour. Time for a nap and a long, lazy dinner before our night shift starts," Grant said absently.

"Yes." She shot him a glance. All week long he'd talked about those naps. They'd been patrolling at night, going home to bed at dawn, collecting cages of live animals in the afternoon and returning to his cabin for a "nap." Only somehow they never got around to closing their eyes.

Grant, she'd discovered, had an insatiable sex drive and an infinitely creative imagination. No secrets were safe with the man. Once he'd woken her by mercilessly tickling her feet. On another occasion he'd rubbed her entire body with warm, soothing baby oil. They'd made love on his kitchen table while two venison steaks had burned. They'd made love in the sunshine. He'd taken her with a fierce speed that had left her breathless and trembling. He'd taken her with slow, lazy humor, making her laugh, teasing her until pleasure had turned to torment and she had become a wanton aggressor, which seemed to be exactly what he wanted.

As a lover he was pure giver. And as a man . . . she couldn't live this close with him without seeing the terrible loneliness in his dark eyes sometimes. She saw love in his smile every time she walked into a room. She saw impatience when she was only seconds later than he thought she should be. They bickered, teased, talked. They loved as if each moment was all there was.

It seemed to be all he wanted. Kathryn was letting the love affair happen, watching herself climb higher and higher on the rungs of a ladder that led nowhere. Her instincts promised her he needed her, but what if her instincts weren't worth horseradish? In the meantime, she'd never worked so physically hard in her life, all for creatures who snarled in her face if she dared get close. Her minks valued freedom; they didn't care who they hurt to get it.

Her head repeatedly warned her that Grant was the same. Her heart insisted it took time, and love, to tame a wild creature. All she could do was give. She'd waited a lifetime for a man worth opening up for, giving to, risking with. She told herself she could outwait a man afraid of commitment, and she tried not to think. That wasn't so hard. Living these crazy hours with so much to do, she had little time to think.

Only arriving at his place this afternoon was different. "Grant!" She saw the three men in the yard before he did—and they had Baby. Each had a long leather leash wrapped around her neck, and it was taking all three men to hold her. The normally sweet, placid bloodhound was gnashing and snarling. "Hurry—they're trying to steal her!"

"No, Kate." Grant vaulted out of the passenger door before she'd even stopped the truck. The men, spotting him, were suddenly all shouting and talking at once. One, a tall blonde, kept waving a cloth in front of Baby's nose. Each time he did it, the dog all but went mad.

Grant had gone over to talk to the men, but he was doing nothing to stop them. Leaping from the truck, Kathryn was ready to kill the entire male species. She surged toward Baby until Grant's hand closed on her wrist. "Don't touch her. Not now, Kate. She's not a pet now—she knows there's work to do."

"But—"

"I've worked with these men before and so has Baby. There's a child lost. The Perkins girl. She was playing by the creek with her brother two hours ago. She wandered off."

It was the last thing he said to her. So much happened so fast. Grant went inside and returned minutes later, wearing ankle boots and a strange leather harness strapped to his shoulders. He attached the leashed ropes to the harness, taking control of Baby. The three men were still talking all at once—one was the child's father, another an uncle, the third . . . she had no idea. Family and neighbors were out looking for the little girl. The problem was that her last tracks had been by the creek.

Kathryn was abruptly sick to her stomach. The creek was generally shallow, but there were places where it thinned out into deep pools, places where the current was swift. "And how can Baby track her in the water?" she asked despairingly.

The men were headed back for their trucks. "That bloodhound could track a lost plane in the sky," the blonde told her. "Water's never stopped that mutt before, and, besides, she'd climb from here to hell for Grant."

"You have to know bloodhounds," the dark-haired man told her. "Nothing'll control that dog once she's got a scent."

"Baby?" The dog who moaned with despair for a piece of pizza? she thought incredulously.

"She went nuts over finding a teenager two years back. Grant slipped over some rocks. She dragged him all of fifty feet. He had to be stitched up right fine when it was over with. You look at how heavy he is, and you'll know just how strong that instinct is in the dog to sniff out a scent."

"He'll find Janey," the blond man consoled the other. "You know damn well he won't come back without her."

When they were gone, Kathryn stood in the yard, rubbing her damp palms uneasily on her jeans. They'd offered to take her with them; she'd wanted to go. Her urge was to be involved, to be with the child's mother, to help if she could. She couldn't erase the picture of the men waiting for Grant from her mind. He was taking charge of the dog. They assumed he'd jump to help, and he had. He could be hurt. Her heart ached with the possibility. She wanted to respond as readily as he had, to be the first to see him return, to know he was all right, to know if and when he'd found the little one.

Only she couldn't go. People who knew the land and the child were already involved. They were honestly in a position to help. However frustrating, helping people sometimes meant staying out of their way. The back of Grant's truck was filled with traps of live creatures, and someone had to feed more than a hundred minks tonight. She had no idea how long Grant would be.

By dusk he still hadn't returned. She'd tried to eat dinner, but couldn't. By ten she was worried sick; it was pitch-black, and her teeth were clamped together as she headed for the truck again. Grant had done it the other nights—reached in a gloved hand and pulled out a wriggling, snapping creature from each trap. She was scared of getting bitten. She was scared of wolves and bobcats. She was terrified Grant was hurt, and she was slowly but surely getting furious.

Irresponsible, was he? Taking just what he wanted and needed from life? Uncaring and uncommitted? He'd have had her believe all those things. They'd made love, but he carefully never mentioned futures. He only believed in the here and now, in taking the moment.

Poppycock.

He cared enough to risk life and limb for a child he didn't even know. He took charge, and he didn't have to think; it was his nature. His capacity and need for love were equally enormous—but Kate was beginning to despair that the damn lummox would ever figure that out.

It took her three hours before the cages in his truck were empty. She tasted metal on her tongue each time she reached into a trap. Teeth clamped on her glove more than once. She never got used to it. Each time she dropped a creature inside a fence, she saw the lustrous soft fur of a mink, its beady eyes waiting. Beauty...and cruelty. The price for her choices? Kathryn doubted she'd ever eat again.

She patrolled until 5:00 a.m. the silly popgun at her side, daring any predator to come close. None did. Other nights she'd seen a fox, woodchuck, predator owls. This night she was happy not to be tested.

Just before six she opened Grant's cabin door, exhausted, hoping desperately to find him at home and knowing she wouldn't. He'd have found her if he'd been home, and every hour that ticked by couldn't mean good news for the lost little girl.

It was an absurd time to bake, but she couldn't just sit there, and she certainly couldn't sleep. The predawn morning was crisp and chill, and the cabin too empty and dark without him. She lit a lantern and started a small fire. After putting a pot of coffee on the coals, she fussed with flour, baking powder and salt—squaw bread, he'd called the recipe. She didn't care what it was called. She just wanted him home, on his terms, on any terms.

She was pulling the hot bread out of the oven when the back door opened. Gray dawn silhouetted Grant's slumped shoulders, and exhaustion rimmed his dark eyes. She was so glad to see him she almost cried.

"You found her?"

He nodded. "She's all right. Badly mosquito bitten, scratched and shook up to beat the band, but she's all right."

"Baby—"

"Gets a steak. Pronto. And if you'll take care of that, I'll go back out and feed your minks." He made an instinctive move to halt her rush forward. "That'll save, honey. That seven-year-old had to find every mud hill and dirty hole in the entire Upper Peninsula. Not to be crude, but I don't smell the best."

"You idiot. Do you think I care?" She rose on tiptoe to give him a swift crush of a kiss. He reeked of mud and sweat. She'd never loved him more. "And I've already fed the minks."

"You what?"

She took charge. She started a hot bath—showers were for men who still had the strength to stand—found the largest venison steak in the freezer for Baby, poured coffee, ordered Grant out of his clothes and started scrounging for his first-aid supplies when she got a good look at his face and the cut on his arm.

In less than fifteen minutes he was immersed in water to his chest, a cup of coffee in one hand and a half-devoured piece of her squaw bread in the other. Kathryn perched herself on the side of the claw-footed tub with a first-aid tube in her hand.

"Dammit, Kate, a man's bath is sacred. And I don't need any of that stuff."

"Close your eyes," she ordered. His forehead looked as if he'd tackled with a brier bush. She began smearing disinfectant on his cuts. He winced like a defiant child. "Now turn this way."

"No. And I don't believe you handled all those critters. You knew damn well I'd be home—so they'd have gone hungry for a few hours. It wouldn't have killed them. You could have been bitten. I told you before—"

Yes. He'd told her a lot of things before. She paid no attention. The scrape on his thigh had gone right through his jeans. A spot on his forearm was turning black and blue. He was scratched, bitten, bruised. His shoulder had a cut that should probably be stitched—she doubted she could sell him on that, but it was certainly getting a bandage. She interrupted him with a crisp, "And you're going immediately to bed after this." She heard his barking laugh, but just continued looking at him.

"Dammit, Kate, could you quit yelling at me long enough so I could finish yelling at you?"

She leaned back, a wry smile on her lips. "We do seem to have a small problem here."

"Yes. You're bossy."

"I'm bossy? You're the one belting out all these orders."

"So are you."

She nodded, then grabbed a towel for him to step onto. "I've noticed it before—we're both of a type, Grant. Managers, people who have to give orders and organize and take charge or they go nuts. Disgusting traits, really, but you can't take the tart out of a lemon. If you'll remember, though, you're supposed to be the laid-back type." She stood up and wagged a finger at him. "You've got two minutes to be back on the bed in there, or I'm coming back in after you."

She'd caught something in his eyes—something of surprise, something of anger. He didn't like to think of himself as being a managerial type. She ignored his glare, closed the door on the bathroom and started pulling back the covers on the bed.

Seconds later he stalked out of the bathroom stark naked. "I *am* the laid-back type," he informed her instantly, as though five minutes hadn't elapsed since their conversation.

"Of course you are." Patting his fanny, she directed him back to bed as if he were two years old. When he got there, he crashed like an ox, and his shoulders and back yielded like putty as she rubbed him down.

"You're the only manager in this twosome."

"Yes, Grant."

"You're the one who needs to take charge of things, and you're welcome to it. I got all that out of my system years ago."

"I know you did."

"I'm not apologizing to anyone for dropping out, Kate, or for living my own life exactly the way I want to. If you think I miss the constant pressure and tension—"

"And challenge. And that gritty feeling of victory when you've beaten them all, and won, and done it

your way. Or that feeling when a problem's too big
and there's no possible solution—but there is, and you
find it, just you—"

"Shut up, Kathryn."

"You're still living it," she whispered, kneading his
flesh with her fingers. She'd promised herself not to
force this talk; it wasn't fair to kick a man when he was
down. She'd given freely because she wanted to, not
because she ever expected a return from Grant. But
she had to try just once. Maybe because he was vulnerable and exhausted right now, he'd have to see.

"You think you're free, Grant?" she whispered.
Lovingly she worked to soothe his tight shoulder
muscles. "You think you've thrown off responsibility, your own need for challenge and commitment?
But I've been living with you, lover. You chose a hard
life where you could have chosen luxuries—because
you needed that challenge. You tracked a child tonight. You just did it. When everyone else was scared
she was lost or dead, you didn't care—you just moved.
I've watched you take on my minks. All that sweat and
hard work and stink of the darned creatures, but you
loved it. Because it was a problem. Who the heck do
you think you're kidding? It would never matter where
you lived, a ghetto or Antarctica—you'd still thrive on
challenge, you'd still find something to take charge
of—"

She found herself on her back, staring up into furious dark eyes and lips thinned in a hard line. "Shut
up, Kate," she whispered.

He didn't smile. "Believe me, honey, that was my line."

"You're tired."

"It might have occurred to you after a night like this that arguing philosophies could wait for another time."

His strong leg was thrown over her. His shoulders had twice her own breadth, three times her physical power. His hair was damp and unruly, and she gently touched the cheek of her wild man. "That's why. Because you were tired. I thought you'd have to listen."

"We do damn good, Kate. When we don't talk."

He couldn't have hurt her more. "Funny. You make me talk all the time."

"Because I care what happens to you."

"Only I'm not supposed to care back? It's okay for you to question my values, my feelings. But not okay for me to ask you if you're so very sure of yours?"

He hadn't slept in twenty-four hours. His every muscle and bone ached from the strain of controlling a seventy-five-pound dog for the past twelve hours. He was still tense from worrying about the child, and before that he'd carted the weight of cages over miles of rough terrain in the afternoon. He damn well didn't want to talk.

His mouth crushed hers with an anger he didn't want to feel. If there were other ways to control her witch's tongue, he knew the one that mattered. She was in the mood to rock boats? Kate could be persuaded into other moods.

She was susceptible to kisses in that hollow between throat and collar-bone. The insides of her thighs sometimes couldn't bear touching. Her nipples tightened under the gentle-rough flick of a thumb. His hand cupped the soft fur between her legs. He knew exactly what moved Kate.

It took no effort to remove her clothes. She didn't fight him. He began the orchestration as a master. He knew every swell and timbre; he had control. He tuned Kate for perfection, for music she could get lost in. If his touch was rough, she often vibrated with rough urgency, took fire in it. He wanted the fire.

He needed the fire.

He touched collarbone, thigh, nipple. She lay there, all satin skin. She kissed back, but softly. He whispered. She hushed him with more soft kisses. His fingers slid between her legs...but she didn't curl and tense around him as she should have. She whispered, "I love you, Grant. You give so much. Is it so hard for you to risk taking, to admit that you need, too?"

His mouth sealed hers silent. He delved deeper for the fantasies that touched her. In real life, Kate valued control, pride and strength. But in bed, in her secret core, she liked feeling taken, overpowered, protected. She liked feeling a little wicked. He nipped at her breast, zippered kisses on her abdomen. He rolled her over and let his tongue trail her vertebrae, then back again, his palm sweeping her inner thigh, his tongue sweeping her mouth.

Her breath was coming in shallow gasps. She rained soft kisses on his lips, his cheeks, his jaw. Kisses of softness, not kisses of fire. "I love you," she whispered. "*Love*, Grant."

She was beginning to think he'd never hear her...but he was still for that moment. She shifted so that she was lying bare against his bareness. Her lips dipped to his throat, his heartbeat. "I love your hands because they're your hands, not for what your hands do. I love your mouth, love, but not because of the way you kiss. I love the man. If you're trying to make me climb walls, you can probably make me climb walls, but not for sex, Grant. It's you. I want you."

She was trembling, trying to talk, trying to kiss, trying to remain calm, trying to pretend she was unafraid. Grant's caresses expressed perfection and perception, not feeling. He was as determined to arouse her as he was determined not to care, not to listen. He was cold, and he'd never been cold with her before. Lying bare in his arms, she knew fear. Beneath the layer of skilled lovemaking, she knew she was dealing with anger.

"Kathryn..." If he kissed her any harder, he would have bruised her mouth. "Dammit, what do you want?"

"For you to make love with me."

"I have been."

"No. That was sex. Care for me enough not to do that, would you? Maybe I'd give in. I don't know. I don't want to know. Maybe I just need to believe that I wouldn't. But if you're honestly not in the mood to make love, let's just curl up. I'll hold you. You're tired. I need to hold you."

Would she never stop talking? He was so damned tired. Her fingers touched his cheek, threaded into his hair. Her lips were like honey, sapping the last bit of energy from him. He felt control slip, control he never let go of.

Her breasts rubbed against him. A long, slim leg feathered between his. He'd never meant to hurt her. If she wanted cotton light, he'd have given her cotton light, but it didn't seem a texture she wanted. She wanted ... soul.

A wisp of fine blond hair tickled his abdomen, her intimate kiss on his thigh, the scrape of her fingernail, her sweet mouth ... she gave and kept on giving. That wasn't life. Life was a survival course in toughness, beating out predators, enemies, anger, frustration, never being vulnerable. And he gave in with a desperation that shamed him, a desperation that easily earned the response of her fire. With rawness, fear and exhaustion he reached inside himself and touched the terrible dread of being alone. She was there, arms and legs wrapped around him, whispering encouragement. He'd never come to a woman with less than strength, but he came to Kate less than what he wanted to be. She rewarded him in whispers, with heat, cleaving with abandon, demanding without shame.

Consumed with a wild, fierce need, he took her. Jasmine and damp skin and all her tastes ... he couldn't get enough. He made the sky explode for her, once, twice. He wanted to do it a thousand times.

His body claimed release and took it, and afterward he felt the claw of exhaustion. He fought sleep, still wanting to hold the rainbow. To hold Kate. He needed her.

There was a time in his life when he'd sworn never to need anyone. He was sharply aware that Kate had gotten closer than he'd let any other soul.

Too close.

Nine

———

Twenty miles from Grant's cabin and two miles from any road, there was a small, spring-fed lake. Virgin forest bordered it on three sides, and tall grasses and brush on the other. Bass and bluegill populated the cool blue waters. From hollow logs to a deserted muskrat house, there was abundant shelter for any small mammal. The water was fresh, the earth fertile, and it was here, with Kathryn watching from the distance, that Grant freed the last mink.

The mid-August day was warm, the sky filled with clouds that looked like white tumbleweeds. Arms folded across her chest, Kathryn waited for Grant to make his way back to her. They'd spent the past week scouting out places for the minks.

Engineers couldn't have worked harder. Each site had to support wildlife and had to have the special food and shelter minks needed to survive. Since minks fought to the death for territory, no two could be placed too close, yet a male and female certainly had to be close enough to find each other in the spring. There had to be easy prey for the mink, but hopefully prey he wouldn't have to face too much competition for.

They'd started with a hundred and thirty and had lost nineteen. A hundred and eleven were now free, and Grant's grin reflected the triumph. He threw both arms around Kate's neck and kissed her. "You did it, lady."

"*We* did it."

It was a long drive home. He kept shooting her those quick grins. Her nose had a slight sunburn; she wasn't wearing any makeup. Her boots were dusty, and her hair was loose, tossed up in an abandoned breeze. If she still had a problem sitting still, Kate definitely wasn't the same person she'd been when she'd first arrived. To credit her with serenity might be pushing it, but there was a glow about her, inside and out.

A month ago, the night the child had been lost, they'd come close to an argument. To his relief, Kate had never brought up the issues again. If they didn't share the values she was so worried about, he had at least concentrated hard on showing her what they did share. They'd worked and eaten together and made love and more love. Kate had breathed in a freedom of spirit and had shared it, in laughter and warmth and intimacy. He'd watched her grow and glow, losing the tension that had once been part of her every day. Every change he would have wished for her had happened.

He stopped the truck by the mink site. There was little left to do; they'd taken up the fencing as each mink had been freed. Grant had destroyed the makeshift shelters and filled in the water holes. Kate—being Kate—had planted wild daffodils. Inevitably the earth still looked disturbed, but by spring no one would ever know they'd been there. Three rolls of fencing, from the pens of the last minks they'd just freed, were still standing. "I'll take care of these now," he told her.

"Fine. I'll be up at the cabin."

"Have a pot of coffee waiting?"

"Promise." She grinned.

When he stomped through her door an hour later, he found not only a freshly brewed pot of coffee in the kitchen, but suitcases on the leather couch as well. The smile on his face died. Kathryn was just climbing down from the loft steps with a pile of clothes in her arms. She glanced at him, set the clothes in the suitcase and then crossed to the cupboard for mugs. "Hungry?"

"No."

Easygoing and casual all morning, he suddenly looked tight as a drum. Kathryn poured his coffee and handed him the mug. "I am. I swear I could eat a horse." She added wryly, "But I think I'll settle for a peach. Sure you don't want one?"

"What the devil are those suitcases for?"

"Those?" Her eyes flickered toward the living room.

"Cut it out, Kate."

"You knew I had to go back to Chicago." Her teeth sliced into the tough skin of the peach, sinking into the sweetness inside. Juice spurted on her tongue. "Lord, this is good."

She'd learned to eat again. He took credit for that; he took credit for a lot of the changes in Kate. At the moment he came close to taking the peach from her mouth and hurling it out the window. "When do you plan on leaving?"

"When I always planned on leaving...when the last of the minks were freed. You already knew."

"Specifically?"

"When I get packed and close this place down."

"You can do that in an hour or two."

"Yes," she agreed. He was upset. She took another bite of peach.

"So...you plan to go, just like that. Not even stay a weekend—"

"Weekends at the store are the busiest times. I've pawned off enough responsibility on Bess."

"Fine," he snapped, and then repeated, "Fine. If that's what you want." He fell silent. Dark eyes gripped hers and wouldn't let go.

She turned away and tossed the peach stone into the trash. Her hands were sticky, oddly trembling, when she reached for the pump to rinse them off. Her fingers had barely plucked the towel before it was snatched out of her hands. She was spun around and her chin tilted up before she could catch a breath.

He slammed a kiss on her mouth. Her lips tasted very much like peach and reminded him indelibly of cherries. He caught the shimmer of love in her eyes and closed his own. Blind, he unraveled buttons, pushed away material. He wanted her bare and now.

So she was going? He wanted her gone. He always knew she wouldn't stay, and he wanted to get back to his own life. Alone, where no one was around to upset him all the time, to challenge him, to badger him into shaving off a beard. Alone, where a certain someone wasn't doing things all the time. She was damn dangerous in bed. He would find a woman who was far less dangerous, far more restful.

He'd set out to give her a taste of freedom, and he'd done that. She was talking partnerships and management changes in her store. He knew she'd never go back to the frenetic life-style she'd had before, though. She'd take better care of herself. She noticed things now—like sunlight, like grass. He'd done something good for her, and he felt good about it and was glad she was going. What they'd shared was sweet and good and right, but he knew he'd come damn close to needing her. That close was too close. He needed no one. A man depended on himself. He'd been alone before and had reveled in it . . . and he would again.

Her leaving quick and fast was best. Easiest. Exactly what he wanted.

Kathryn felt him bury his hands in her hair, felt the trembling power of kiss after kiss. Like a sponge, she

absorbed the flavor and scent of him. Her skin was
supple and giving where his touch was rough and ur-
gent. She was bare to his fully clothed when he
scooped her up.

She knew he didn't want to think. She helped him
do exactly what he wanted to do. The leather couch
barely yielded under her slim spine. His mouth traveled over her skin with yearning pressure; his fingers
absorbed the texture of her. He never took off his
shirt. He never once gave her the chance to breathe
until he was inside her body and the fierce, wild pulse
of rhythm had taken them both.

Then he slowed. His eyes opened on hers, liquid
black, full of desperation, despair. "Damn you,
Kate," he whispered.

The weight of him was so familiar, so welcome. She
took him into her softness, wrapped him up in limbs
and warmth and kisses like silk. If tears burned, she
kept her eyes closed. None escaped. She gave him
everything he'd taught her—all the emotions. Love,
frustration, anger, need, sweetness. Freedom . . . and
freedom was an emotion. He'd taught her that, too.

When it was done, he rained kisses on her cheek, her
temples, her closed eyes. His lips were buried in her
hair when he whispered suddenly, fiercely, "Don't go,
Kate. Stay here. Live with me."

It was hard to talk for the lump in her throat. Finally she managed a soft but definite, "No."

* * *

Bess flipped the quarter, caught it and peeked at the gleam of metal on her hand. "Heads." Triumph glinted in her eyes. "You get to handle Mrs. Baker."

"You're sure that isn't a two-headed quarter?"

"I only wish. I got stuck with her twice last week."

Kathryn smiled, swinging out of her desk chair. It was the first of October, and the crispness of fall was in the air. Dressed in a jewel plaid skirt and magenta sweater, she sent a glowering look at her partner's sassy grin. "I really feel," she said firmly, "that we could come up with a far more professional, intelligent, mature way of handling this than flipping a coin."

"So do I. Are you willing to drown the woman?"

"I'm considering it." She strode to the door. The store was crowded on a Thursday afternoon. Customers milled around coats and suits to the display of wool slacks and hand-knit sweaters near the front door—where she found Mrs. Baker. The woman had a fine habit of wasting an afternoon trying on clothes, leaving them in shambles and never buying a thing. It would have helped if the lady hadn't been bent on believing she was a ten when she was a clear-cut fourteen on her slim days.

Kathryn plastered a smile in place. "May I help you?"

Tact and patience came with the territory. Mrs. Baker liked red, the worst of colors for her. By the time the lady had clothes piled in her arms and was aimed for the dressing room, Kathryn took some satisfaction in knowing that the styles, colors and sizes would at least complement the customer's full-bodied looks...even if the wretched woman didn't buy anything.

She was just straightening the sweaters when movement through the glass store windows caught her attention. A black Maserati jammed on its brakes directly in front of the no parking zone in front of the store. The car was pure posh, waxed to a fancy gleam with accents of chrome and black leather.

Her eyes narrowed when the man climbed out of the car. He was dressed in a navy blue suit, new and custom tailored to suit his broad-shouldered frame. His chin had a smooth shave, and his hair was brushed back in a clean, tamed style. He ducked his head back into the car before striding for the store doors. When he pushed open the door, he had one hand on the neck of a champagne bottle, and a dozen orchids in an open box in the other.

Her heart fluttered as his gaze impatiently whisked over the crowd of faces. His eyes finally found hers and locked in. The sophisticated image only worked so far, she thought fleetingly. Grant's snapping black eyes would never be tame. His smile was wicked, and his shoulders were still caveman primitive. One could only subdue a natural savage to a point. The desire in his eyes was bright, bold, naked. Anyone on earth could have seen it, and that desire came striding toward her as if the man who possessed it would have mowed down mountains if they'd gotten in his way.

"Hi." He swooped down and claimed her mouth—just a swift kiss. Just hello, and a "dammit I've wanted you and why the hell are there all these people here" kiss. It was as if he'd seen her yesterday and took for granted seeing her tomorrow. He lifted his head, glanced irritably at the customers staring at him, and then back at her. "I need you alone. Preferably in the next three and a half seconds."

She shepherded him into her office in an even three. He had no idea how huge the hope in her heart was. Two-months-of-waiting huge. For two months of loneliness and desperate silence, hope had filled her soul, because there was nothing else there.

Grant dropped the champagne and orchids on her desk and forgot them. If he'd barged back into her life like a freight train, he had eased down to slow motion now. His eyes skimmed her office.

She leaned back against the desk, unable to help smiling. When he pushed a hand through his hair, tameness went out the window. A very powerful man looked ready to come apart at the seams. Sure sophistication, dominant determination, the strength of confidence and purpose...all of it reduced to something else when he looked at her. Emotion sang between them, so rich and thick she could have touched it. He wasn't nearly as sure as he wanted her to believe.

"I love you, Kate." His tenor filled her small office. "And I damn well knew I loved you long before this."

"Yes."

"I missed you like hell."

"Yes."

"You knew I would."

"Yes." She felt like laughing with sheer exhilaration. First he braced his hands on his hips and then he folded them around his chest and then he just let them hang. She'd always been the one who had to do something with her hands. Now it was him.

"I've thought...about a lot of things. I've thought...about what a baby of ours would look like. I want you to have my baby, Kathryn Price."

"I would love to have your baby," she said softly.

Some of the tension eased in his shoulders. His tenor picked up speed with a snowball's momentum, allowing her no chance to interrupt. "I've been wrong for a long time about a lot of things. We're going to do this your way, Kate. All your way. In town, with a white picket fence around the house if you want it. No roughing it, everything nice. I know what that cabin of mine looked like, so I don't know what you thought, but believe me, I have money. More than enough to give you all the security you could possibly want. We can live exactly where you want, exactly how you want. I'd rather have a house than an apartment because of Baby, but—"

"And because of the kids."

He breathed again. "And because of our kids." He waited, unsure why she'd ducked her head. Her hair was still the color of sunshine; she still had a duchess's profile. When she finally tipped her head back, her eyes were as blue as love...and shimmering with unshed tears. Fear rocked through him with stunning speed.

Loss of hope rocked through her with equal power. "Damn you," she said achingly. "You don't know how hard I hoped you'd come...but not like this. How could you so completely misunderstand everything?"

"Misunderstand—"

Only pride kept her chin steady. "We spent two months teaching those minks to be free. At the time it seemed so ironic—that they had to be taught to be free, that they had to be taught to cope in their own natural environment—"

"Kate, the last thing I want to talk about is minks."

"We're not talking about minks. We're talking about what you taught me, about freedom. About risks worth taking. And I hoped—I've hoped for two long months—that you'd learned something, too, about that balance of freedom and risk, about what you really wanted and needed in your own life. How could you ever think I wanted to put you in a cage?" Before she could change her mind, she jammed the orchid box back in his hands, and plopped the cold bottle of champagne on top of it. "You wouldn't survive five minutes in a white picket cage, Grant. Don't you know that?"

"Cage?" He wouldn't understand the woman as long as he lived. "I'm trying to tell you that I'm willing to play the game completely, totally on your terms, dammit. That I love you."

"I love you, too." She pulled open the door. Her pain was frozen in her white face, in a regal profile that showed no emotion. "More than you know. Get out, Grant. Just get out of my life."

Furious black eyes pinned hers at the door. "If you think for one minute that I'll be back..."

Tears stung like needles the minute he was gone.

The last pair of stockings was hung over the shower rail when she heard the bang of a fist on her apartment door. She hurriedly dried her hands and belted her quilted robe. It was ten o'clock in the evening and typical of late October—a cold drizzle spattered against her windows. It was that kind of night. She was expecting no one, but would settle for anyone who had a remotely human face.

The pounding on the other side of her door was loud enough to wake the dead, and it didn't exactly reassure her about the human quality of the species on the other side. Rising on bare toes, she peeked through the peephole.

She considered having a heart attack. Instead she opened the door... and nearly had her face knocked with an angry fist for her trouble. The vagrant standing in her hall wore holey jeans, a disgraceful black sweatshirt and a belligerent expression. His hair glistened with rain; his chin needed a shave.

He'd brought his big guns this time, she thought fleetingly. Baby was at his side, panting and looking despondent, and a freezing cold brown bag was shoved in her hands before she could stop it. She looked inside and found twenty pounds of frozen cherries.

"Couldn't find any fresh ones. Don't tell me I can't come in, Kate, because I'm going to talk to you."

It seemed politic to move aside, since Grant strode in as if he were prepared to mow down armies. Kathryn lagged at the door long enough to bend down and give Baby a hug and kiss. "I missed you, too," she whispered. A honey-colored tail immediately knocked the *Wall Street Journal* from the entrance table.

She picked it up and then padded barefoot after her unexpected guest. A lonely, gloomy night abruptly turned volatile. She leaned her cheek against the cool smooth wall, watching him pace. His cheeks were ruddy from cold; his eyes had the black shine of the night's bleak rain. If she'd met him in a dark alley, she most certainly would have run. If she'd met him in a boardroom, she'd probably have run as well. He would probably have been at home in either, but the broad shoulders, sexy dark eyes and jeans were definitely out of place next to her peaches and pastels.

"You look beautiful," he mentioned.

She figured that was obligatory, one of those things he'd reminded himself to say as fast as possible so he wouldn't forget. She already knew he found her beautiful. It wasn't necessary for him to say it. "Thank you."

"Your place is beautiful, too."

"Thank you again." Her voice was wary, soft.

"I've got a job, Kate."

"Oh?" Baby padded over by the window and crashed with a sleepy thump. Her master didn't. Kathryn saw the bleak pallor beneath his weathered color, the tired hollows beneath his eyes. It had been three weeks since she'd seen him. The way he looked measured how long those weeks had been. "Sit down," she urged him.

He didn't. "Korfan's the name of the place. The owner died a few months ago, and his son doesn't know how to run it. I hired on as a consultant. I don't know a damn thing about metallurgy and never did."

He waited, as if expecting her to say something, but he hadn't said anything she needed to hear yet. Magazines were strewn all over the coffee table. She moved to straighten them, and then to pull the draperies on the cold night and light a side lamp. Her heart had the same pitter-patter beat of the rain. Her damn heart should know better than to build up hope again, but hearts were such irrational things.

Grant went on, his words tripping over themselves in an effort to get said. "I don't have to know anything about metallurgy, but the principles of making a small company work still apply. The kid doesn't have the right people, for openers. In small industry, there's no room for deadweight. You've got to tighten costs, upgrade efficiency and have a product or service that's able to compete against the big boys because it's irreplaceable in some way. Dammit, Kate, would you quit moving and settle somewhere? *Anywhere*."

She smiled. The first real smile she'd felt in a million years. It was coming. She could feel it, measure it in the growing excitement in his voice. Belatedly she realized that she was still holding the bag of frozen cherries. No wonder her fingers were growing numb.

Grant wasn't exactly sure why he kept talking—the last thing on his mind was consulting work—except that he'd been wanting to share it with Kate for a week. "Korfan's was one choice. Bartholomew's was another. The guy who owns that is an engineer, and a brilliant one, but he's got the management skills of a dunce. He's looking for someone to sort through the chaff, make his larger plant into something he can manage. He knows exactly where he's weak, and that's a plus. All he needs is to have someone come in temporarily, set up right-hand men he can trust, reorganize a less complicated management system—"

"But you could hardly take on both jobs," Kathryn said smoothly.

"Bartholomew's willing to wait until winter. I figure in a year I could have them both straightened around." He dragged a hand through his hair, wishing Kate would remove that soft smile from her face and say something. Preferably something meaningful. He also wished she'd stop moving.

"Those weren't the only offers you had, were they?"

"No." It still surprised him. "I knew I'd built up a fair reputation with my own companies, but that was a while back. When I walked into Korfan's, I expected to be shown the door. I told the guy flat out—this is who I am, this is what I've done, this is what I think I can do for you. I told him he could pay me three percent of his increased profits that first year or he didn't have to pay me at all. I told him take it or leave it, and the fool took it. Kathryn—"

She'd disappeared around a corner. He trailed her, passing a tall, delicate vase of dried peach wildflowers that probably would have toppled over if he breathed on it. Her kitchen area was much the same—all delicate pastels and feminine textures. He couldn't escape the smell of jasmine anywhere. The last thing he expected to find was her lifting a chilled bottle of champagne from her refrigerator.

"I was listening," she assured him.

"No, you weren't." He took some badly needed air into his lungs. Leaning back against her counter, he watched the minx struggle with the metal clasp covering the cork. That smile of hers was gaining momentum, radiating the special brand of feminine superiority that reeked of smugness. He was still suffering, and she was busy being self-satisfied.

"I thought . . . I was so sure . . . you never gave one hoot in hell if I was gainfully employed." His tone was suddenly, dangerously quiet.

"Nope. Never." She laughed, a sound lighter than bells. "You finally figured that out?"

The cork popped and soared to the ceiling. First white fog whispered out of the bottle, then a trail of foam. She reached for glasses just as she felt two arms slide around her waist from behind. His lips nuzzled aside her robe collar and bit tenderly into vulnerable white skin. She tried to keep talking. "I cared that you found something you wanted to do with your life, something that excited you, challenged you. You taught me balance, Grant, but it was missing just as terribly in your own life. Darn it, I never want to see you strung out on a pressure treadmill, but all you'd traded for that was a different kind of cage. I wanted you free. Free to love me, and until you took the risk, accepted that ambition and drive were part of you— Grant! There's no possible way I can manage this if you don't stop doing that."

"There's not another minx on earth who can talk as much as you, Kate."

Her chilled champagne had been waiting for him since August. They were her best crystal glasses, but he didn't seem to care. He swung her around and placed a kiss on her mouth that could have scorched an iceberg. Her balance reeled from the taste of him.

She'd waited so long for this. Her arms swung around his neck, and she held on and held on. She felt the shudder pass through his skin, become absorbed in hers. Her rough diamond was touch and strong. A little arrogant—he hadn't lost that in their months apart. And incredibly vulnerable—she saw it in his eyes. He lifted his mouth abruptly. "Have you been kissing any other men like this?"

"I haven't been kissing any other men at all, idiot. I've been waiting for you to get smart, and I darn well thought it would take you forever." She pushed back his hair where he'd shoveled his hand through it. She had the right to the possessive gesture.

"I was never not smart, Kate. It just took me a little time to understand that I couldn't live without you." He touched her cheek, not smiling. "It wasn't a joke when you left. Nothing was the same, nothing was right."

"I know." Her heart ached, remembering. His mouth found hers, and she yielded up the last of loneliness and fear. He was here. He really was here, and unquestioningly sure of what he wanted, what he needed in his life.

Her quilted robe was long-sleeved and floor-length. Beneath that, she wore blue panties. About the same time he discovered that, Kathryn shivered violently. He had no intention of letting the duchess catch cold. When they reached her bedroom, he turned on a lamp and enjoyed the intimate perusal of her private dominion for a moment. But not for long. Other intimacies were the sweeter priority. He pulled her panties off; she didn't need them.

"We have a small problem here," she murmured.

"We have no problems, Kathryn."

"I just thought it might be nice if you took off a few clothes, too."

His sweatshirt immediately graced her bureau. His jeans graced her floor. The rest of his clothes formed puddles in a direct path to her bed. His eyes held hers as he undressed. He didn't give a damn if he ripped his clothes, his eyes told her. He didn't give a damn if there were a hurricane outside, or a world war, or if the sky caved in. He had a woman to claim. A minx who had driven him half mad, trying to figure out how to win her.

"We're going to go slowly, Kate," he said gruffly.

She was sure he meant that, but his slowness didn't last very long. His hand touched her bare skin, he felt the length of her to the length of him—and urgency claimed them both.

She had so much to tell him: that she had no intention of stealing his freedom, that he could make his life his own way. She held him accountable only for being honest with himself. He could make mistakes. She'd be there. He could still have his north woods; she knew that was part of him. She'd make sure he never got lost in that workaholic pressure cooker that had once sent him off alone.

She told him all of that with her lips, her hands, her body. She worshiped his skin. She savored his taste. She lured him to soft fire, by rubbing where he loved being rubbed and teasing where he was sensitive. She knew he loved her wild. He had no idea how wild she could be, now that he was here, now that she knew he was permanently part of her life and that terror of loneliness was gone. Only Grant had ever understood her.

He had so much to tell her. He'd been arrogant and interfering in her life when his own wasn't better than a glass house. He had thank-yous to give her, for patience. For waiting. He wanted to tell her that he wanted her free, always. Free to do what she wanted, free to feel, free to explore change and challenge and life. In every way he wanted her to feel free with him, that there was nothing she couldn't do when they were together.

He told her that with his mouth, his hands, his body. All of her, from fingertips to toes, he loved. Every inch of her flesh had to be touched, loved, caressed. Now. It wouldn't wait. She wouldn't wait. The taste of her filled him. Her scent, the sound of her sweet, rough breathing, and then she started whispering to him....

He saw her eyes, wild soft. He climbed on and in. Her fingers clutched the hair on his chest, and he kept seeing her eyes, open, honest, hot...and so full of love. Her legs wrapped around him, sealing him tight and hard inside her. Rhythms of heat, like a firecracker just before exploding, and still her eyes were open, loving him, inviting him. He felt that private part of her tense, those tiny muscles contract as her breath grew shallow, and she was so irresistibly helpless... he'd never loved her more. If he could have willed it, he would have had her pleasure last for centuries. At least a lifetime. Her joy triggered his, though, and then it was done, and he was holding her so tight she probably couldn't breathe; he didn't care.

It took time to climb back down. She felt him ease his weight off her, but then he simply dragged her on top of him and held her that way. His hand reached out to switch off the light. Silvery rain still spattered against the windows. It was a nasty world outside, the best of worlds in. She felt the tap of his palm on her fanny.

"All right, you. Whose fault is it I came at you like a madman?"

"Mine," she acknowledged.

"Next time we're going slow."

She smiled, her cheek in his chest hair—it tickled. Both of their bodies were damp, satin damp. "I love you," she mentioned.

"I love you, too. Desperately, Kate." His finger lifted a strand of her hair and examined it in the darkness. The strand was like sunlight, even at night. That wasn't logical. "You like gold bands, or baubles?" he asked lightly.

"Gold bands."

"I'd rather buy you diamonds."

"I don't need diamonds."

"I want to buy you diamonds."

She roused from sleepiness long enough to take a small, distinct bite out of his shoulder. He took his punishment like a man; she had to give him that. He kissed her tenderly on the lips and cuddled her closer.

"I also want your babies, Kathryn," he said sternly.

"This particular evening, that might be more than a possibility. I'm not prepared."

"Good." He pulled her comforter over both of them, and they were both silent for a time.

"You think our minks are all right?" she whispered.

"I think they're free," he replied quietly. "Which could well mean that they're wet, cold, hungry and in danger. But they are free, Kate. Don't you ever regret what you did, ever."

"The people in town thought I was crazy."

"So?"

"I couldn't make any other choice," she said softly. "You have to reach out, for whatever's there. You have to take the risks. I lived too long in a cage, Grant. I so terribly wanted to feel safe."

"You are safe. Nothing's going to hurt you again, Kate. Nothing, I promise you."

It would. He was wrong. The difference was that he was part of her life; he would be there. If she were the one who had to take all the initial risks, it was to have exactly what mattered now. Independence could be measured in two. Self-reliance didn't have to be lonely. Alone had never proved anything at all.

"Grant?" she murmured.

"Hmm?"

"You're into threesomes?"

"What?"

"We're not alone."

"Down!" Grant ordered Baby.

The bloodhound buried her head in her paws, as if that effectively hid the rest of her seventy-five pounds.

"Let her be," Kathryn whispered.

"She's *not* sleeping with us."

Kathryn smiled in the darkness while he escorted Baby into the other room. The bloodhound would undoubtedly be back on the bed by morning. She didn't mind. Baby had always shown a gift for tact and sensitivity; she wouldn't show up again for several hours. Time enough.

A female had to let a man think he was in total control on occasion. Grant, for instance, undoubtedly thought he'd tamed a lady some months back.

She knew all along who'd been tamed and untamed.

Grant was in the mood for slow, languid love when he came back to bed. So was Kate. One of the most fantastic things he'd ever taught her was laziness. Slowly, lazily, languidly, she made sure he knew how much, how tremendously, she adored him.

Her wild man thrived on tenderness. She came alive at his touch.

And they were three in a bed by morning.

*　*　*　*　*

 # Silhouette Desire

COMING NEXT MONTH

367 ADAM'S STORY—Annette Broadrick

Adam St. Clair fell in love with Caitlin Moran after she saved his life. Could he convince her that a future together was in the cards? A sequel to Annette Broadrick's *Return to Yesterday*, #360.

368 ANY PIRATE IN A STORM—Suzanne Carey

As the vice-president of her family corporation, Amanda Yates was fair plunder for Royce Austin. Royce planned on a takeover, and he had more than business on his mind!

369 FOREVER MINE—Selwyn Marie Young

Blair Mackenzie took some time off to go camping and escape her problems. But once she met up with mountain man Dominic Masters, trouble was never far behind.

370 PARTNERS FOR LIFE—Helen R. Myers

Kendall and Braden had been the best of friends and a dynamic police team—until love got in the way. Now, no amount of danger could keep them from dreams too long denied.

371 JASON'S TOUCH—Sheryl Flournoy

Jason was a man of many talents, theft not the least of them, according to Corey. But after one look at Corey, Jason was more than willing to become a thief of hearts.

372 ONE TOUGH HOMBRE—Joan Hohl

Though from different worlds, J.B. and Nicole were two of a kind—and it didn't take long for them to learn that opposites attract.
This novel features characters you've met in Joan Hohl's acclaimed trilogy for Desire.

FREE!
Never Before Published

Silhouette Desire™
by Stephanie James!

A year ago she left for the city. Now he's come to claim her back. Read about it in SAXON'S LADY, available exclusively through this offer. This book will not be sold through retail stores.

To participate in this exciting offer, collect three proof-of-purchase coupons from the back pages of July and August Desire titles. Mail in the three coupons plus $1.00 for postage and handling ($1.25 in Canada) to reserve your copy of this unique book. This special offer expires October 31, 1987.

Mail to: Silhouette Reader Service

In the U.S.A.
901 Fuhrmann Blvd.
P.O. Box 1397
Buffalo, N.Y. 14240

In Canada
P.O. Box 609
Fort Erie, Ontario
L2A 9Z9

Please send me my special copy of SAXON'S LADY. I have enclosed the three Desire coupons required and $1.00 for postage and handling ($1.25 in Canada) along with this order form. (Please Print)

NAME _____

ADDRESS _____

CITY _____

STATE/PROV. _____ ZIP/POSTAL CODE _____

SIGNATURE _____

This offer is limited to one order per household.   DPOP(L)-A-1